"Get up," said Cummings. "I don't want to kill you sitting down."

"It didn't bother you to shoot a man in the back," Slocum said.

"You're different, Slocum. Get up. We'll make it a fair fight."

"Go to hell, where you belong."

Slocum wondered if he was playing a fool's game. Cummings was good. He knew that. And all things being equal, a man standing certainly had the advantage over a man sitting down. He saw Cummings's right hand twitch, and he knew that the man was getting nervous.

"Get up, Slocum," said Cummings. He was no longer smiling.

"Jasper," said Slocum. "You ain't worth standing up for."

Cummings's hand went like a blur for his revolver . . .

DON'T MISS THESE
ALL-ACTION WESTERN SERIES
FROM THE BERKLEY PUBLISHING GROUP

THE GUNSMITH by J. R. Roberts
Clint Adams was a legend among lawmen, outlaws, and ladies.
They called him . . . the Gunsmith.

LONGARM by Tabor Evans
The popular long-running series about U.S. Deputy Marshal
Long—his life, his loves, his fight for justice.

SLOCUM by Jake Logan
Today's longest-running action Western. John Slocum rides a
deadly trail of hot blood and cold steel.

JAKE LOGAN

SLOCUM AND THE TOWN BOSS

JOVE BOOKS, NEW YORK

If you purchased this book without a cover, you should be aware that this book is stolen property. It was reported as "unsold and destroyed" to the publisher, and neither the author nor the publisher has received any payment for this "stripped book."

SLOCUM AND THE TOWN BOSS

A Jove Book / published by arrangement with
the author

PRINTING HISTORY
Jove edition / March 1997

All rights reserved.
Copyright © 1997 by Jove Publications, Inc.
This book may not be reproduced in whole
or in part, by mimeograph or any other means,
without permission. For information address:
The Berkley Publishing Group, 200 Madison Avenue,
New York, New York 10016.

The Putnam Berkley World Wide Web site address is
http://www.berkley.com/berkley

ISBN: 0-515-12030-8

A JOVE BOOK®
Jove Books are published by The Berkley Publishing Group,
200 Madison Avenue, New York, New York 10016.
JOVE and the "J" design are trademarks
belonging to Jove Publications, Inc.

PRINTED IN THE UNITED STATES OF AMERICA

10 9 8 7 6 5 4 3 2 1

1

Slocum hauled back on the reins, bringing the heavy freight wagon to a dusty stop in front of Hogan's Freight Company on the main street of Joshville. It was already getting dark, and Slocum was late. As he set the brake, a small crowd of curious locals, mostly from the saloons that lined the street, began gathering around him. He wasn't surprised at that. He had expected it, for there was blood on the side of his head, and his shirt was torn and dirty. The Colt revolver was missing from the holster at his side. An old bearded codger with a wad of tobacco in his slack jaw stepped up close to the wagon and squinted at Slocum.

"Hey, sonny," he said, "You look like hell. What happened to you?"

Slocum eased himself down out of the wagon with a groan just as Hogan, sweating from the long day and from the anxiety of waiting for an overdue wagon, stepped out the front door of the freight office. The big man crossed his arms over his chest and scowled down at Slocum there by the wagon.

"That's a good question," Hogan said. "Let's hear the answer. I hope it's a good one."

Slocum pushed his way through the crowd and stepped up on the board sidewalk to face Hogan. The massive frame of the freight company's owner blocked the doorway.

"Let's go inside," said Slocum.

Hogan stared at him for a moment, then stepped aside, and Slocum walked through the door. Hogan looked over the crowd a moment with a dark frown on his round, red face, then turned and followed Slocum into the office, slamming the door shut behind himself as he stepped inside. Slocum was already at a sideboard washing his face over a bowl of water.

"Well?" said Hogan.

"I made the delivery all right over to Wagon Gap," said Slocum, "and I collected the money too. On the way back I was waylaid by five men. The bastards got the best of me."

"I guess that means they got the money too," said Hogan.

"Well, that's what they were after," said Slocum. "Yeah, they got it."

Hogan walked up close to Slocum's back as Slocum wiped at his face and the side of his head with a towel.

"How'd they get the drop on you anyhow? Hell, I hired you because you're supposed to be some kind of gunfighter."

Slocum turned to face Hogan.

"I didn't hire on as no gunfighter," he said. "You hired me to haul freight. That's all. You ain't paying gunfighter wages. Even so, I'd have used my gun if I'd had a fighting chance, but I ain't no damn fool.''

Hogan reached up, taking Slocum by the hair, tilting his head to one side to get a better look at the wound.

"Well," he said, "at least you put up some kind of fight. They got your gun too, huh?"

"Yeah," Slocum grumbled. "Sons of bitches. And I didn't put up no fight at all. Hell, Hogan, I never told you I was a gunfighter. I don't know what gave you that idea in the first place."

Hogan moved around to the far side of his desk and sat down heavily in his big chair. He took a deep breath and heaved a long sigh.

"Okay. What happened?" he asked.

Slocum pulled a straight chair up close to the front of the desk and dropped down into the seat.

"You know that sharp curve just at the top of the grade west of town?"

"Yeah," said Hogan. "I know it."

"They were waiting there," said Slocum. "Four of them. Guns ready. I was busy fighting the team at the top of the grade. Just made the curve and there they were. The fifth one jumped in the back of the wagon and hit me on the side of the head. I don't know where the hell he come from. When I woke up, they was gone, the money was gone, and my six-gun was gone too."

"You recognize any of them?" Hogan asked.

"No," said Slocum, "but if I ever see one of the four again, I'll know him. The one that come up behind me— I didn't get a look at him."

"Damn it all, John," said Hogan, "those bastards are going to put me out of business if I don't find a way to stop them."

The door opened just then, and a potbellied man with a handlebar mustache and wearing a badge on the left side of his black vest stepped into the office. He was breathing hard from the effort of walking to the freight office.

"What's happened here?" he asked.

"Nothing's happened here, Brady" said Hogan. "My driver got robbed out on the road on Bald Knob by five masked men. I don't suppose there's anything you can do about it, though."

"What do you mean by that?" said Brady. "I am the town marshal. Course I can do something about it. It's my job. But you got to report the crime to me. How do you expect me to do anything if you don't report the crime to me?"

"I'd have gotten around to it sooner or later," said Hogan. "Hell, Slocum just now told me what happened. I just didn't figure there was any hurry to tell you about it. This is the fifth time my drivers have been robbed on Bald Knob, and you ain't done nothing about it yet. Besides, I didn't know which saloon to look for you in."

"I been working on the robberies," said the marshal. "These things takes time. And by the way, asshole, it's past my regular office hours. If I want to have a drink in a saloon, that's my business. Now suppose you tell me what happened."

Slocum told the tale again, just as he had told it to Hogan. Brady listened attentively, occasionally nodding and murmuring to himself. When Slocum was done, Brady got up to leave.

"I'll ride out there first thing in the morning and see if they left any trail to follow," he said. "In the meantime, Slocum, you see any of those men around, you let me know right away."

"Sure," said Slocum, and the marshal lumbered, huffing and puffing, out of the office.

"He won't find anything," said Hogan. "He ain't worth a shit."

"Say, Boss," said Slocum. "I've got an idea. If you want to hear it."

"Hell," said Hogan, "I'm desperate. I'll listen to anything."

Slocum wondered why he had opened his big mouth before he had taken time to consider his own thoughts. He ought to just walk away from this mess. He knew that. It wasn't his problem. He hadn't intended to drive Hogan's freight wagons as a lifetime career anyhow. But Hogan, for all his gruff talk, had been fair with him, and the man was really in trouble. And more than that, the five road agents had pissed Slocum off.

He didn't mind getting whipped in a fair fight, but they had surprised him, and one of them had even hit him from behind. Then they had stolen his Colt. They had insulted and humiliated him, and he didn't like the thought of letting them get away with that. Anyway, he had already opened his big mouth. He had no choice. He was compelled to tell Hogan his idea.

"Fire me," Slocum said, "and use another driver."

"What?"

"You heard me right. I'll go out of here cussing you with you yelling right back at me in front of the whole damn town."

"Why the hell would I want to do that?" said Hogan. "You were right. If it happened like you said, there wasn't a damn thing you could have done to stop it. Hell, Wild Bill Hickok couldn't have stopped it."

"You fire me in front of the whole town," said Slocum. "What we won't tell them is that I'll be on those gunfighter wages we talked about."

"I don't recall talking about gunfighter wages," said

Hogan, "and I can't afford them. Especially not on top of a driver's wages. I'm telling you, John, these bandits have about got me busted."

"I'll wait for my pay till after we've got them whipped," said Slocum.

Hogan rubbed his chin, thinking.

"What else can you do?" Slocum added.

"What if we don't whip them?" Hogan said. "And what if I never get my money back? I won't be able to pay you."

"That's my worry," said Slocum, "and it's my job."

"So you're no gunfighter, huh?"

"I never said that either."

"What's the plan?" Hogan asked.

"We'll make a big show of you firing me, and you and me won't even talk to each other again out in public without cussing. As far as the bandits or anyone else is concerned, that'll put me clean out of the picture. Then first thing in the morning, send out the regular load just like always. I know where those bastards like to waylay the wagons, but this time I'll be hid out there myself. I'll take them by surprise instead of the other way around."

"It would still be five against one," said Hogan.

"That'll be my worry too," Slocum said.

"Well, it just might work," said Hogan. "All right, by God, let's try it."

Hogan stood up and stretched his arm out across the desk toward Slocum, and Slocum took the big hammy hand for a quick shake. It was as official as the deal needed to be between two men who trusted one another.

Outside, some of the crowd that had gathered earlier was still standing around speculating among themselves about what might have happened to the freight wagon, when the door to the freight office was suddenly jerked open from inside, and Slocum backed out shaking his fist.

"No one could have done any better out there than what I did," he shouted. "Hell, all I hired on to do was just drive your damn wagon anyhow. That's all. Just drive. I didn't hire on to fight no damn road agents."

"You're a goddamned coward," Hogan yelled, "and a lazy bum to boot. Get on the hell out of here and don't come back. It makes me sick to look at you."

"You still owe me money," Slocum called out, and just then several coins came flying through the door to land in the dusty street. Slocum turned to retrieve them as Hogan slammed the door shut from inside. The old bearded codger picked up a coin just as Slocum looked toward him. Slocum gave him a hard stare, and the old man, regret in his eyes, handed the coin over to Slocum. Slocum stuffed all of the coins in a pocket of his jeans.

"Goddamn bastard," he muttered, and turned to angle across the street in the direction of the White Horse Saloon. He heard someone call his name, and he looked over his right shoulder to see Curly Joe Haywood, the young cowboy, running in his direction. Slocum stood and waited until Haywood came up beside him.

"What's up?" Haywood asked.

"I just got fired," said Slocum. "Want a drink?"

Without waiting for Haywood's answer, Slocum resumed his walk.

Haywood fell in step. "Sure," he said. "How come you got fired?"

"I got robbed along the road on the way back to town today," Slocum said. "Hogan blames me. I guess he thinks that I should have got myself killed trying to protect his damn money. Hell, Curly Joe, there was five of them. Nothing I could do. Not a damn thing.''

''I don't see how he can blame you for that,'' said Curly Joe.

''Well, he did. Son of a bitch.''

The two men reached the front door of the White Horse and walked inside. It was still early in the evening and the crowd inside was small. Slocum threw his money out in front of himself on top of the bar.

''A bottle of bourbon and two glasses,'' he said.

''No,'' said Curly Joe. ''If it's all right with you, I'll just have myself a beer.''

''Suit yourself,'' said Slocum. Then he turned back to the bartender. ''Give me one of them good cigars.''

The bartender took the money, and Slocum took his cigar, bottle, and glass to a nearby table and sat down. Curly Joe followed with his glass of beer.

''What're you going to do now?'' Curly Joe asked.

''Hell,'' said Slocum, pouring whiskey into his glass, ''I don't know. Hang around till my money runs out, I guess. Maybe I'll get to watch old Hogan lose his ass. Maybe I'll find another job. Something always seems to turn up.''

As he tossed down his drink, he felt a little guilty lying to Curly Joe, for he liked the young cowboy. But then, Slocum knew that there was only one way to keep a secret, and that was to keep it from everyone. Besides, it was his first real opportunity to play the role he had set up for himself, and he was going to have to get used to playing it. He struck a match and lit the cigar.

''I don't think there's any jobs wanting out at the Running R,'' said Curly Joe, ''but I'll ask old Toby if you want me to.''

''No,'' said Slocum. He poured himself another drink.

"I don't want to chase no damn cows. Not just now. Thanks anyhow. Hey, when I get really low on cash, maybe I'll change my tune."

"Just let me know, pard," said Curly Joe. He lifted his beer glass for a long sip. Lowering the glass, he saw a group of four men enter the saloon. "Uh, oh," he said.

Slocum followed Curly Joe's gaze to the front door and saw Harrison Gould coming into the room. With Gould were three strong-arm men. Slocum knew that Gould was the mayor of Joshville, and that he was in the middle of a heated and occasionally violent political campaign for his job. His opponent, Tobias Reed, was the owner of the Running R and Curly Joe's boss. Walking toward the bar, Gould paused to look down at Slocum.

"Heard you lost your job, Slocum," he said. "That's too bad."

"Word travels fast," said Slocum.

"It does in Joshville," said Gould. "Guess you'll be leaving town then. Jobs are pretty scarce here."

"Maybe," said Slocum. "Maybe not. I ain't broke yet."

"You ain't fixing to get into politics, are you?" Gould asked, glancing at Curly Joe. " 'Cause if you are, it looks like you're joining up with the wrong side."

"Hell," said Slocum, "I'm just having a drink with a friend. That's all. I don't give a damn who's mayor of this jerkwater town."

Gould threw his head back for a hearty laugh.

"That's a good attitude, Slocum," he said. "Hang onto it, and you'll be all right. Come on, boys." He led his three toughs on over to the bar.

"Old Gould didn't especially like seeing you sitting here with me," said Curly Joe.

"I'll sit with anyone I want to," said Slocum. "This country ain't worth much, but that's all right. It's free."

"Not according to Gould, it ain't. He don't think that Toby's got any right to run against him, and he don't think that any of us has got any right supporting Toby. Hell, most of the boys don't know nothing about politics anyhow. We're just punchers who work for Toby. Anyhow, Gould don't like it."

Slocum tossed down another whiskey.

"Well, it ain't my concern. I ain't supporting no one," he said. "I don't give a shit for politics. If I don't find another job pretty soon, I won't even be able to support myself. Speaking of jobs, what're you doing in town so late in the middle of the week? Ain't you got to work in the morning?"

"Aw, Toby give me the day off 'cause I worked extra last weekend."

"You mean, you ain't got to go back to the ranch today?"

"Not till tomorrow morning," Curly Joe said. Then he leaned across the table toward Slocum and smiled slyly. Lowering his voice, he said, "What do you say the two of us go on upstairs and find Jessie and Francine? Do us both some good." He grinned, leaned back, and finished off his beer.

"Oh, I don't know," said Slocum, taking a sip of whiskey. "Someone might be with them already."

"Hell," said Curly Joe, "Someone might not too. Let's go find out. Besides, ole Jessie likes you. I know she does. She told me so."

Slocum wasn't in the habit of frequenting whores. He took pride in the fact that he didn't have to resort to that to get what he wanted. But Curly Joe sure was anxious. And then, Slocum told himself, it would fit right in with the picture he was trying to create of himself as a man disgruntled by his recent firing. Grumbling, drinking, and whoring around. It all fit.

"Well, hell," he said. "Why not? On second thought, that sounds like a pretty damn good idea after all."

2

Curly Joe knocked lightly on the door at first, but when he got no answer, he pounded. The voice that finally came from inside the room was grumpy.

"Who is it?"

"It's me. Curly Joe. Open up."

"Goddamn," came the response. "Do you know what time it is? And it's my day off."

"Sure I know what time it is, honey, more or less, but it's my day off too, and I sure do hate to waste it just only getting drunk. Come on. Open the door, will you?"

At last the door was opened just a bit, and Slocum could see nothing but frazzled hair and one sleepy blue eye peering out.

"There's two of you," said Francine. "Damn it, cowboy, what the hell do you want?"

"We want you to get Jessie to come and join us," said Curly Joe. "You know ole Slocum here, don't you?"

"Oh. Yeah," she said. "Hi, Slocum." She stepped back and opened the door wider. "Well, hell, come on in." She turned her back on the two men and walked across the room to a table for a hairbrush. Slocum, being the last one in, shut the door behind him.

He took note of the shape of Francine's body beneath the thin robe she wore. She was small, but she had some fine curves on her frame, and her round ass shook prettily as she stroked her hair with the brush. At last she tossed down the brush and turned back around to face the two men. The scowl was gone, and her face wore a fresh and coy smile.

"Sit down," she said. "Make yourselves comfortable. I see you brought your own bottle, so have a drink while I go round up Jessie. Give us girls just a few minutes, will you?"

"Sure," said Curly Joe. "We ain't going no place."

"Take your time," said Slocum, pouring himself another drink. Francine left the room swinging her hips, and Slocum thought that Curly Joe's idea was seeming better with each moment. He took a sip and enjoyed the feeling of the brown whiskey burning its way down his throat.

"Ain't she something?" Curly Joe asked.

"She's something, all right," Slocum agreed.

"So is Jessie," said Curly Joe. "And Jessie likes you. She told me so."

"Yeah," said Slocum. "So you said. We'll see how much she likes me here in a few minutes."

"Yeah. We'll see. You won't be disappointed."

When Francine at last came back into the room, her face was bright. She'd washed it and repainted it, Slocum realized. Jessie walked in close behind her. She had long, dark hair and big, dark brown eyes. She was a bigger woman than Francine, but just as shapely, and the robe she wore revealed even more of her bountiful body than did Francine's.

Just inside the room, she shut the door, leaning back against it. She looked at Slocum, and her full lips twisted into a half smile.

"Hi, Johnny," she said, in a low, husky voice. "I've been wondering when you'd come around to see me."

Francine sat on Curly Joe's lap, took the hat off his head and tossed it aside, then put her arms over his shoulders and leaned forward to kiss him full on the lips. Curly Joe murmured his pleasure out loud through the kiss. He reached around her waist with both arms, pulling her closer into his body, as she opened her lips and shot her tongue deep into his mouth.

Ignoring them, Slocum stared back at Jessie, who had not moved away from the door. He emptied his glass and set it and the bottle aside. Then he snuffed out his cigar in a nearby ashtray.

Francine was sliding her hands underneath Curly Joe's shirt.

Slocum pulled off his boots and dropped them beside the chair. He stood up and removed his vest and then his shirt, throwing them over the back of the chair. He looked at Jessie, still leaning back against the door, still staring at him seductively with the same half smile.

He walked over to her and took her by the shoulders. Stepping in close, he pressed her against the door with his body, and he crushed her lips with his. He felt his cock rising in his jeans, and he knew that she could feel it too, for she thrust her hips forward in response to the throbbing down there.

She reached down, forcing both her hands in between their tightly pressed together bodies in order to unfasten his jeans, then allowed them to drop down around his ankles. Slocum pushed the robe over the edge of Jessie's shoulders, and it slid easily to the floor. Her sumptuous bare breasts were then pressed against his chest, and she took his swollen cock in both her hands and squeezed it hard, thrilling as it bucked and jerked, as if it were trying to break loose from her tight grip.

"I think it needs to be tamed," she said.

"I'm glad you didn't say broke," said Slocum. "Think you can do it?"

She smiled at him, and slowly bent her knees. As she moved herself lower and lower, first her breasts and then her tongue stroked his body along the way. Then she was on her knees, and she was still holding tight to the shaft of the menacing cock. It was right before her eyes.

She reached down with one hand to disengage Slocum from his jeans. Then suddenly she shot out her tongue, giving his cock head a flick, and the thing tried to buck loose from her grip once more. She held on, though, and gave it a slower wet lick. She ran laps around the head with her tongue, and suddenly, she sucked the whole cock into her mouth and clamped her lips tightly around it. Slocum gasped in spite of himself.

Behind him, Francine stood legs spread and naked on the floor, leaning forward and resting her elbows on the bed. Curly Joe was right behind her. He had dropped his trousers down around his boots. Too anxious to even bother undressing, he was driving his swollen rod into her from behind. Slocum could hear the slapping of Curly Joe's happy flesh against the bare round ass of Francine.

He could hear it, but he wasn't interested. He was much too involved with his own ecstasies, as Jessie moved her head back and forth, sliding her wet, warm lips up and down the length of his shaft. The urge to begin driving into her built up inside Slocum, and not wanting to pound himself against her face, he reached down for her. Taking her head in his hands, he gently urged her away from the pulsing cock and lifted her to her feet.

Again she leaned back against the door, and she lifted one leg. Slocum bent his knees, slipped an arm under the lifted leg, and drove his rod upward, sliding it into her slippery cunt.

"Ah, God," she cried out, as she felt her depths filling up with his hard and throbbing flesh. Slocum reached for her other leg. Then he lifted her by both her thighs, straightening his own legs, and she was wrapped around him, both arms and legs, and riding him for all she was worth.

"Oh, damn," she said. "Damn, that's good."

Slocum thought that it was interesting for a short ride, but still, he was not doing the thrusting. He walked over to the opposite side of the bed from where Curly Joe was still driving into Francine from the rear. Jessie still bounced up and down on his cock. Holding her tight, he climbed onto the bed, falling forward. As Jessie landed on her back with Slocum on top of her, his weight drove him even deeper into her soft channel, and she cried out in a joy that was almost pain.

Slocum began driving in earnest now. He had her where he wanted her. Her legs, which had been clamped hard around his waist, now loosened and she spread them wide, the better to take him in. She thrust upward with her hips each time he humped down and into her, and their rhythm was perfect. Their two bodies worked in exact harmony. It was like a frantic but perfect dance.

"I'm coming," shouted Francine.

"Oh, lordy," said Curly Joe. "Me too."

"Ah, ah, ah."

"Oh, oh, oh."

Curly Joe spurted again and again far into the squishy pleasure tunnel, and Francine felt some of the warm juice running down the inside of her right thigh. Curly Joe at last stood still, gasping for breath, and he allowed his satisfied cock to slip out of the hole. Francine straightened up and turned to face him. She threw her arms around his neck and kissed him on the lips, shoving her tongue almost into his throat.

"Maybe we can take time now to get these clothes off of you," she said, and she helped him out of his shirt. He scooted around on his feet until he could sit on the edge of the bed, and she knelt to pull off his boots and get his legs loose from his jeans. Then she put her hands on the inside of his thighs and slid them slowly up to his wet cock.

"Oooh," she said. "This needs to be cleaned up."

She sucked it into her mouth and rolled it around in there, cleaning it of all the commingled juices, hers and his. Curly Joe threw back his head, moaning in great pleasure.

Just then Jessie felt the ecstatic release swell inside her to the breaking point, and she began to moan, a long, low moan gradually increasing in volume. Slocum drove harder and faster, and then he too felt the dam burst, and he began to gush forth a great load, emptying himself in spurts into the dark and damp depths of Jessie's wonderful cunt.

Curly Joe and Francine were by this time disentangled and were sitting on their side of the bed watching the action with fascination. Slocum thrust one last time and then relaxed, allowing the weight of his whole body to press Jessie down into the mattress, and allowing his much exercised cock to soften slowly inside her.

"Damn," said Curly Joe. "I think I need some of that whiskey now."

Francine jumped up and fetched the bottle over. She took a slug herself and handed the bottle to Curly Joe. He took a drink and held it over toward Slocum, but Slocum hadn't moved.

"Hey, John, boy, you ain't dead there, are you?" he asked.

3

Slocum was just finishing his breakfast in the local cafe when Gould and his toughs walked in. Gould stopped just inside the doorway, and the three toughs stopped obediently just behind him. Slocum could see Gould's eyes fasten on him for a moment. Then the mayor turned his head to the right and leaned back slightly. An obliging tough leaned forward, giving the mayor his ear. Gould spoke low, the tough nodded his head, and Gould turned to leave, all three of his boys stepping aside to give him plenty of room for his departure.

With Gould gone, the three stared hard at Slocum, then one, tall with red hair, took a sideways step toward a table. The other two followed, and they all sat down. Slocum tried to ignore them, but they continued to stare at him. Clearly, they were up to no good. Damn, Slocum, thought, I got enough worries without getting caught up in local politics.

He drained his coffee cup, shoved back his chair, and stood up to leave. He made it to the counter to pay his bill, all right, but on his way to the door, he tripped over a size-twelve boot that had been stuck out into his path by the redhead, and went sprawling.

Quickly he rolled over onto his back, reaching for the Colt at his side. It had been an automatic reaction, a reflex. There was no Colt there. There was nothing. The goddamned freight wagon bandit had taken it. Finding himself doubly embarrassed, Slocum looked up to see all three of Gould's men on their feet, six-guns in their hands, grinning wide and looking down at him.

"Why ain't you wearing no gun, boy?" asked the redhead, who was not nearly as old as Slocum.

"Aw, hell, Red," said the shortest of the three, "don't you recall? Bandits got his gun."

"Yeah," said the third. "Just took it away from him. He didn't even put up no fight at all. That's the way I heard it."

"Is that right, Slocum?" Red asked. "Is that what happened to your gun?"

Slocum drew in a deep breath. This was no time for him to be telling Red and the other two just what he thought of them and their chicken-shit tactics.

"That's right," he said. He started to get back up to his feet, moving slowly and deliberately, not giving the shits any excuse to shoot. "So there's no reason for the three of you to be holding six-guns on me. Even if you wanted to kill me, which you probably don't, 'cause I can't think of no reason for it, you sure wouldn't want to shoot an unarmed man, the three of you together like that, in a whole room full of witnesses. You wouldn't want to do that."

He was standing now and dusting off the front of his shirt.

"I'll just be on my way," he said, and, his heart

pounding, wondering if one of the three was fool enough to shoot, he turned his back on them and headed for the door. Red looked at his two sidekicks, shoved his own gun back into the holster at his side, and gave them a nod to follow him. They holstered their own weapons and fell back in line. Red's long strides took him close up behind Slocum by the time Slocum had hit the street.

From an upstairs window of the White Horse across the street, a scantily clad Francine looked out and saw what was happening.

"Curly Joe," she said. "Come here."

Still naked, Curly Joe jumped up from the bed and ran over to stand beside Francine. "What?" he said. "What is it?" But before Francine could answer, he had seen for himself. "Oh, shit," he said, and he ran for his britches.

Back out in the street, Red took longer steps, almost walking on Slocum's heels, and then he deliberately swung his long left leg out and around, causing Slocum to trip once again.

Slocum fell hard, and a cloud of dust rose around him. He lay still a moment, working to control his anger. Then, covered with street dust, he turned over again to face his tormentors. This time they were not smiling, nor were they holding their revolvers ready. They stood side by side looking down on him with grim expressions on their ugly faces. Slocum looked straight at Red.

"That's a bad habit you've got there," Slocum said in a calm voice.

"Hell," said Red, "you just seem to keep getting in my way."

Again Slocum stood up slowly, careful not to give any one of the three an excuse to swing a fist or draw a gun.

"What's this all about?" he said. "I don't even know you."

"That's right," said Red, "and we don't want to know you. We want you to get your ass out of town."

"You got no business here," said the short one. "You ain't even got a job here no more. So move on."

"Now," said the third.

"Look," said Slocum, "I done told your boss that I ain't interested in politics. I ain't involved—"

"We don't want no conversation," said Red. "We're just telling you to move on. That's all."

Right then Curly Joe burst out the front door of the White Horse to Slocum's rear. He had managed to pull on his jeans and to strap on his revolver, but he wore no shirt or boots. Slocum saw the six eyes shift to focus on something just to his own right, and then out of the corner of his own eye, he saw Curly Joe come to a stop just beside him.

"Howdy, pard," said Curly Joe. "You got some kind of problem with these here?"

"Oh, I don't think so," said Slocum. "Not now. I think you just raised the odds enough to scare these chicken shits off."

"I wouldn't be so damn sure if I was you," said Red. "I see your buddy's packing a gun too."

"Ain't no gunplay called for here," said Slocum.

Red's whole attention was focused on Curly Joe by this time, and he had taken on the look of a man ready to go for his gun. Slocum had seen that look often enough before, and he recognized it. Then he saw the other two shift their attention toward Curly Joe. He had never seen Curly Joe use his gun and had no idea how proficient the cowboy might be, but if he was like most punchers, he probably wasn't worth a shit. And he was

facing three men. Slocum, himself unarmed, was standing too far away to make any kind of move on the gunmen. He longed for his Colt. He noticed the marshal
standing on the board sidewalk back behind the three
gunmen, just standing there like a curious onlooker.

"Brady," he called out. "God damn you. Are you
just going to stand there and let this happen?"

"Stay out of this, Brady," said Red, without taking
his eyes off Curly Joe. "Go for it, Haywood. You going
to go for it?"

"No," said Slocum. "He ain't. Not against three of
you. Brady?" He got no response from the marshal.
"Curly Joe," he said, "unbuckle your belt and let it
drop."

"Aw, I don't know about that," said Curly Joe.

"Just do it, goddamn it," snapped Slocum.

Reluctantly, Curly Joe reached for the buckle of his
gunbelt and unfastened it. He let it fall to the ground.

"All right," said Slocum. "Follow me."

Slowly he sidestepped to his right, and Curly Joe did
likewise, moving away from the gun. The three armed
men followed with their eyes. A good distance away
from Curly Joe's gun, Slocum stopped.

"Now," he said, "if you're just dying for a fight, toss
your irons over there with his and let's get it going."

Red hesitated, but he did notice that a large crowd
had gathered on both sides of the street. Slocum had him
buffaloed, and he knew it. He couldn't let the townfolks
think that he was afraid of Slocum. The other two looked
at him, waiting for his response.

"Let's take them, boys," he said, and he unbuckled
his gunbelt. His cronies followed his example, and then
they all walked toward where Slocum and Curly Joe
stood waiting.

"Hell, it's still three against two," someone shouted from the crowd.

"That's all right," Curly Joe called out. "It looks like an even match to me. Come on, you moronic jackasses. Come on."

Slocum decided that if any of the three was really dangerous, it would be Red. Besides, Red had tripped him twice in one morning in front of other folks, and Slocum really wanted to whip Red's ass. He figured that he would move quickly on Red as soon as they were close enough. Within a couple of long strides, the three stopped and raised their fists in some semblance of a pugilistic stance. Slocum looked Red in the eyes.

"You know," he said, "your red head reminds me of the red ass of a blue tick hound."

Red roared and moved in fast with a wide swinging right, which Slocum easily sidestepped. Then he reached out with his own left leg, kicking both of Red's legs out from under him. Red came down hard on his back, all the air knocked out of his lungs, and Slocum turned quickly on the next nearest opponent. It was the smallest of the three.

"Come on, Short Shit," said Slocum.

Short Shit moved in swinging wild but fast, and a couple of his blows pounded Slocum's ribs. Slocum slapped his open palms hard against Short Shit's ears, and the little man screamed and fell to his knees, grabbing his head in both hands. Slocum glanced at his two victims, both still down, then looked over to see how Curly Joe was doing.

The cowboy and the third tough were engaged in a pretty good slugging match with one another. Curly Joe caught a left hook on the side of the head that staggered him, but he managed to duck under the right that followed, and when he came back up, he delivered a powerful uppercut to his opponent's chin. The man staggered back a few steps. Curly Joe followed quickly, not wanting to give him time to recover.

He delivered a sharp left jab to the man's nose, snapping his head back. Then another just like it. He moved in close with a left and then a right to the midsection. The man doubled over, and Curly Joe raised a knee hard and fast that finished the job. The thug straightened up and fell over backwards. He was out cold.

"How you doing there, John?" said Curly Joe.

Short Shit was still holding his ears and crying, and Red, having at last gotten some air back into his lungs, was trying to sit up. Slocum grabbed Red's shirtfront and pulled him to his feet, then drove a right deep into Red's gut, once again emptying the lungs of air. Red slumped like a flour sack, and Slocum let him drop.

"You think they've had enough?" he asked Curly Joe.

"I think so," the cowboy said. "Hey. You want a drink?"

"I thought you had to get back to the ranch this morning," Slocum said.

"I do," said Curly Joe, "and I will in just a bit. Right now I want a drink."

"Yeah, me too," said Slocum.

Francine met them at the front door of the White Horse, a bottle of good bourbon in hand, and led them back upstairs to the room where they had spent the night. Jessie was there, and she was just filling a tub with hot water.

"I thought you boys might need a bath after what you just went through," she said.

"That ain't a bad idea," said Slocum. He reached into

his pocket for a cigar, only to discover that it had been smashed beyond use. He tossed it aside.

"I'll bring you a fresh one," said Francine. "I was just going back down for some glasses anyhow."

She left the room, and Slocum looked at the inviting tub of water.

"Who goes first?" he asked.

"I'll let you," said Curly Joe. "I'll just wait for Francine to get back. Besides, you took out two of them to my one."

Slocum started pulling off his clothes, and he was just settling down into the tub when Francine returned with the glasses and a cigar. Jessie took the cigar, stuck it in Slocum's mouth, and struck a match to light it with. Francine poured four drinks and passed them around.

Slocum eased himself down into the water while puffing his cigar. He took the cigar out of his mouth and sipped the whiskey.

"Ah," he said. "That's good."

Jessie dipped a rag into the water and started to bathe Slocum's face. He leaned his head back against the rim of the tub and let her do it. It was pleasant.

"You know," she said, "those three ain't going to let it go. They been lording it over folks in this town for so long, they can't afford to let you two get away with what you done to them."

"Hell," said Curly Joe, "what're they going to do? They just found out that the three of them can't handle just the two of us."

"They can slip up behind you and shoot you in the back," said Francine.

"And don't think they won't," said Jessie. "They've done it before. And they ain't the only ones that Gould has on his payroll either."

"That's right," said Francine. "They're just the ones that he keeps close beside himself all the time. At least he did up until now."

"You've got to get yourself a gun," said Curly Joe, giving Slocum a serious look.

"Yeah," said Slocum. He thought about his secret job for Hogan. He really didn't want to be bothered with this local political bullshit or the need for revenge of three small-town toughs. "I might ought to relocate myself too," he added.

"Well," said Curly Joe, "you might be right about that. I'd hate to see you go, but then, you ain't likely to be safe in Joshville after today. That's for sure. Where would you go, pardner?"

"Oh, I don't know," Slocum said. "I might just move over to Wagon Gap and lay around there for a while. What about you?"

"Hell," said Curly Joe, "I'll be okay. I'll just stay the hell out of town, that's all. Long as I'm out at the ranch, I'll be plenty safe. This town bunch won't dare come out to the Running R."

Jessie had already washed Slocum's back, chest, and belly, and now she reached lower in front. Slocum felt his cock rise to attention at her strokes. He looked at her smiling face.

"Aw, you ain't hurt none," she said.

Slocum smiled.

"Hey," said Curly Joe, "I just thought of something. We been worrying about our own selves, John, but what about these here girls? You don't suppose those nasty bastards would try to take it out on them, do you?"

"Hell," said Jessie, "don't worry about us girls. We can take care of ourselves."

"Besides," said Francine, "we ain't done nothing to make anyone mad at us. Have we?"

When Slocum stood up, his rod was also standing. Jessie started to dry him with a towel, and Curly Joe started pulling off his own shirt in preparation for his turn in the tub.

"Look at it this way," he said. "Gould and his men are down on me because my boss is running against Gould for mayor of Joshville. Them three jumped Slocum here just because they seen us drinking together. Now you tell me if you girls have done anything to piss them off. Y'all have sure done more than just have a drink with us."

"Curly Joe's right," said Slocum. Jessie stroked his cock slowly, and he started moving with her toward the bed. "We'll talk about it a little later, though," he said.

4

"I've got an idea," said Curly Joe. He and Slocum and the two girls were all lying naked in bed together, all once more very satisfied. "You want to hear it?"

"Shoot," said Slocum.

"He done shot," said Francine. "A hell of a big load too." She stroked his limp cock lovingly.

"Well," said Curly Joe, "there's a line shack out on the ranch. I stayed out there last winter, and it's in pretty good shape. We could all of us move out there, at least until we figure out what to do with ourselves. What do you say?"

"What would your boss say?" Slocum asked.

"Hell," said Curly Joe, "Toby'd go along. You're all in trouble because of Gould, and Toby's trying to bump old Gould out of the mayor's seat. I think he'd go along."

"I don't know," said Jessie. "Me and Francine make our livings here at the White Horse. Slocum's lost his job. What are we all going to live on? Your wages?"

31

"I've got a little cash," said Slocum. "We'll live on what we've got until we figure out our next move. I'm still thinking about Wagon Gap. And I reckon you two will do all right anywhere you wind up."

"Yeah," said Curly Joe. "It'd just be temporary. Just to get the three of you out of town for right now to keep you safe from Gould's bunch. I wouldn't feel right about leaving you in town. Not after what's happened here today."

Francine sat up and looked at Jessie with a worried expression on her face.

"Maybe they're right, Jessie," she said. "I am kind of scared."

"Let's pack up and get out of town," said Jessie.

"We'll all go together," said Curly Joe. "Are y'all ready?"

"Well," said Francine, "we ought to put our clothes on first."

Once the two women started getting all their things together, Slocum and Curly Joe discovered that they were going to need a wagon in order to make the move. Slocum thought about Hogan, but he quickly dismissed that thought. If he was going to keep his new job for Hogan a secret, he couldn't afford to be seen driving a borrowed freight wagon. After all, he and Hogan were supposed to be on the outs.

Following some discussion, it was decided that Curly Joe could make a run out to the Running R, tell his boss what had happened there in town, get permission for the four of them to use the line shack, and borrow a wagon to use for the move.

Because they weren't at all sure that Francine and Jessie would be safe from the wrath of Gould and his boys, Slocum would stay with the girls until Curly Joe returned with the wagon. Before Curly Joe left town, Slocum went to his own room for his few belongings, including his Winchester rifle. Once he had that in hand, he felt better.

"Where the hell you been?" snapped Toby Reed from his front porch as Curly Joe rode up to the ranch house. The cowboy was late returning from his extra day off, and Reed was a man used to having his orders obeyed. He liked Curly Joe. Curly Joe had been a good hand, and he was a man that Reed trusted. This wasn't at all like him, Reed thought.

Curly Joe reined in his tired mount and swung down out of the saddle. He took off his hat and stepped up toward the porch, looking up at his boss.

"Some things happened in town last night and this morning, Mr. Reed. I got to tell you about them."

"Well, go on," said Reed. "I'm listening."

"You know John Slocum. Worked for Mr. Hogan driving freight?"

"I know who he is," said Reed.

"Well, sir, he got himself fired yesterday. The way I see it, it wasn't John's fault. Five bandits jumped him out on the road, knocked him on the head, and stole the money from his last run. Old Hogan got mad as hell and fired him."

"That's irrational," said Reed, "if that's the whole story, but Hogan's likely working with a short fuse due to all his recent losses."

"Yeah," said Curly Joe. "Well, I went over to the White Horse to have a drink with John, and Gould and them three that tags around with him came in. They started in on John for hanging around with me. Accused him of getting into politics. John said he didn't give a hoot who was mayor, and we thought that was the end of it.

"But we was wrong. This morning they jumped him. I joined in, and we whipped them three pretty good."

Reed nodded his head in understanding.

"I figured you had a pretty damn good reason for being late," he said. "Your face shows that you took a pounding. How do the others look?"

"Worse than me," said Curly Joe, allowing a grin to spread across his face.

"Well, it's my fault you got into that scrape," said Reed. "Take it easy for the rest of the day. You can get back to work tomorrow."

Reed started to turn to go back inside the house, but Curly Joe stopped him short.

"That ain't all of it, Boss," he said.

Reed faced Curly Joe once again, curiosity on his wrinkled old face.

"Go on," he said.

"Well, we figured, after what me and John done to them three, that it ain't going to be safe in town for John. I was kind of hoping that you'd let him move into the old line shack out by Titty Hill. We ain't using it just now and, well, it wouldn't be for long. He's talking about moving on."

Reed wrinkled his brow in thought.

"Well, if he got into trouble in town because of my politics," he said, "I reckon it's the least I can do. All right. He can move in—for a while."

Curly Joe fidgeted with his hat and looked at the ground.

"Can I borrow a wagon to fetch them out there?" he said.

"Them?"

"Well, there's Francine and Jessie too," Curly Joe said. "You see, they kind of took up for us in front of them bastards and, well, being ladies and all, they sure ain't safe in there alone."

"They're whores," said Reed.

"Well, sir, I guess maybe they are," said Curly Joe, "but they didn't charge me and John nothing, and they did kind of stick their necks out for us. John'll likely be taking them along with him to Wagon Gap in just a few days."

Reed paced the length of his porch and back before he stopped to glare down at Curly Joe once more.

"Goddamn," he said. "Two whores and a drifter taking refuge on my ranch."

"Excuse me, Boss," said Curly Joe, "but I think it's just three folks who caught some shit in Joshville for one reason, and that's because they associated with me and that son-of-a-bitch mayor associates me with you."

"You mean that it's my fault they're in trouble," said Reed.

Curly Joe only gave a shrug and looked at the ground.

"All right, Curly Joe," the rancher said, but the deep scowl never left his face. "Take a team and a wagon and move them on out to the line shack."

"Yes, sir, Boss," said Curly Joe, and he turned to run toward the big barn off to his left.

"Curly Joe," Reed snapped, and Curly Joe stopped in his tracks, turned and faced Reed once more.

"Yes, sir?"

"I want you to take Billy along with you. And take one other boy. If anyone in town has a mind to cause trouble, I don't want you to be outnumbered. But you send Billy over here to see me while you're getting the wagon hitched. You hear?"

"Yes, sir," said Curly Joe.

Reed paced again and watched while Curly Joe rode his horse over to the bunkhouse and gave a yell. He saw Billy come to the door, and in another moment Curly Joe rode again toward the barn. Reed stopped watching Curly Joe. He knew that the cowboy would turn his riding horse into the corral, then hitch a team to a wagon. Instead he watched as Billy came trotting toward the house. In another moment, Billy was standing there in front of him.

"Curly Joe said you wanted to see me, Mr. Reed," the cowboy said.

"Curly Joe's getting ready to escort some folks out of Joshville for their own safety," said Reed. "I want you to pick one other man and ride in there with him. Accompany them back just as far as the edge of the ranch. They'll be safe then, and it's nobody's damn business where they go from there. Is that clear?"

"Yes, sir," said Billy. "Mr. Reed?"

"What?"

"You think there might be trouble?"

"It's a possibility," said Reed. "Try to avoid it, but be ready for it if it comes looking for you."

"Yes, sir."

5

There was no trouble in town, but as Curly Joe drove the wagon, with Francine and Jessie on the seat beside him and Slocum and the two Running R cowboys riding alongside on the backs of their horses, Harrison Gould stepped out the front door of the White Horse to stand on the walk and watch their departure. The usual three toughs stood just behind him, glaring hard.

Slocum noticed that Short Shit had cotton balls or some such thing stuffed into his ears. But he also noticed a fourth man standing nearby, not close enough for Slocum to be sure whether the man was a part of the Gould crowd or not. He was a man of medium height, and he was dressed all in black. He was perhaps thirty-five years old, and long stringy strands of blond hair hung down around the sides of his face. His face had a cold look about it, probably because of the nearly colorless eyes. He wore a two-gun belt strapped low around his waist, with the holsters tied down to his thighs.

But what interested Slocum the most was the third

revolver. It was a Colt .45 tucked into the waistband of
the man's trousers, and it had a familiar look about it to
Slocum's eyes. As he rode slowly past the small group,
Slocum tried to swing to the side in order to get a little
closer, and he tried to get a better look at the Colt. He
tried to do all this so that no one would notice his interest, for even if he was right, this was not the time for
any action. He got the best look he could and rode on
out of town. He was glad for the company of the two
extra cowboys.

"How come we let them ride out of here like that?"
said Short Shit, just as soon as the wagon and riders
were out of ear shot.

" 'Cause it ain't the time nor place to go gunning
folks down in the street," said Gould. "That's why.
There's women in that wagon too. What would folks
think? Election's coming up real soon."

"Women," Short Shit snorted. "Couple of goddamned whores, that's what. Hell, my damn ears are still
ringing. That son of a bitch hurt me real bad. I might
go deaf."

"You might," said Red, "if you live long enough.
Now shut up, will you?"

"Well, Smitty," said Gould, "since you're just dying
to do something, follow that wagon and see where they
go. Keep your distance, though. Don't let them see
you."

"Why me?" said Short Shit, who was indeed known
as Smitty. "My ears're hurting me."

"I ain't never heard such crybabying from a growed
man," said the empty-eyed blonde. His voice was low
and almost without expression.

"Just do what the hell you're told, Smitty," said Red,
and Smitty grumbled his way over to a horse standing

patiently at the hitch rail nearby. He took up the reins, mounted, and rode slowly out of town in the wake of the wagon.

"Let's go inside and have a drink," said Gould, and without waiting for any response, he led the way back into the White Horse Saloon. Red and the third member of the ever-present trio followed him. So did the man in black.

Slocum rode up close to the wagon and leaned over in order to speak to Curly Joe above the noise of the wagon wheels and the horses' hooves.

"Curly Joe. You see that old boy dressed in black?"

"Yeah," said Curly Joe. "I seen him."

"Is he one of Gould's bunch?"

"I don't know," said Curly Joe. "I've only seen him around once or twice before. I don't know who he is. Ugly little shit, ain't he?"

"His name is Waters," said Francine. "And he works for Gould all right. I don't know what he does. He's not around town very often, but every time he shows up, he heads right for Gould's office. He's one of them."

"I kind of thought he might be," said Slocum. He decided to keep the rest of his thoughts to himself, thoughts about the third gun in the man's belt, thoughts about the familiar look of the gun and about how the man might have gotten it. But if he was right in his thinking, then where were the other four men, the ones that Slocum was sure he would recognize? Where were they?

Smitty followed the wagon and the three horseback riders until they crossed onto the Running R. Then he turned and headed back toward Joshville. He winced at the loud ringing in his ears, and he longed for an opportunity to kill Slocum. He knew that he would be afraid to meet Slocum face-to-face, man-to-man. Still, he longed to kill him.

It would be nice to be a part of a group that might catch Slocum unawares and surround him, then be the one given the privilege of finishing him off. He wanted to be the one to do it, and he wanted Slocum to know that he was the one, but he sure didn't want it to be a fair fight, man-to-man.

Back in Joshville, Smitty found his cronies inside the White Horse at a table gathered around Gould. The only available chair would put him just to the left of Waters, to the right of Gould. He took it and sat down.

"They went onto the Running R," he said. "I need a glass."

Red shoved a glass toward Smitty, and Smitty reached for the bottle and poured himself a drink. He tossed it down quickly and refilled the glass.

"That's what I figured," said Gould, "but I wanted to be sure."

"Hell," said Smitty, "them was all Running R punchers riding with them. All except that goddamn Slocum. Shit. I knew where they was headed."

Gould frowned at Smitty for an instant, then looked away. "I knew the hands were from the Running R," he said. "I ain't stupid. But they could have been helping Slocum and the girls get the hell out of the territory, not just out to the ranch. I had to be sure."

"I wouldn't bother explaining nothing to Smitty," said Waters. "He's not just stupid. He stinks. He needs a bath."

"I'm afraid to take a bath," said Smitty. "I'm afraid I might get water in my ears. They're hurting and ringing so bad right now, I don't want to take no chances."

Waters shoved his chair back and stood up. "Well, I'm getting out of here," he said. "I can't stand to sit by you."

"You know there was a run this morning," said Gould, his voice low. "Regular schedule. You prepared to take care of it in the usual way?"

"Just the same as always," said Waters, and he touched the brim of his hat, turned, and walked out of the saloon.

Smitty looked into the whiskey in his glass, a long pout on his face. "He hadn't ought to talk to me like that," he said. "Who the hell does he think he is anyway?"

"Oh, shut up," said Gould. "He's right. You do need a bath. Get your own bottle and go sit at another table."

Billy and the other cowboy turned toward the ranch house as soon as they had crossed onto Running R property, and Curly Joe drove the wagon on toward the west.

"Hey," said Francine, "why're they leaving us?"

"We're on the Running R now," said Curly Joe. "We're safe. We don't need them no more."

"Well, how much farther do we have to go?" Francine asked.

"You see that hill off over there?" Curly Joe asked, pointing west. "They call it—well, they call it Titty Hill. I reckon you can see why. The cabin's just on the other side of the hill."

"I still felt better with those other cowboys along," Francine said. "How do you know that Gould's men won't follow us out here?"

"They never have come out here," said Curly Joe.

"Gould and his bunch are scared of the Running R crew. I guess we're just too tough for them."

"One of them did follow us," said Slocum. "Curly Joe's right. When we crossed the line, he turned around and headed back toward town."

Curly Joe looked at Slocum with astonishment. "Hell," he said, "I never seen no one following us."

"It was that short shit," said Slocum.

"That'd be Smitty," Jessie said.

They rode on a little further before Slocum hauled in on his reins. Curly Joe stopped the team.

"What's wrong, John?" he asked.

"Nothing's wrong," said Slocum. "You all are safe now, and you're almost to the shack. Now I know where to find you. You can go on without me. I have something to do. I'll see you later."

If anyone in the wagon wanted to protest, Slocum was gone too fast for them to act on the impulse. He rode away from them toward the southwest. He didn't appear to be going back to town, unless he was taking the long way, and he wasn't headed by the most direct route toward Wagon Gap either. Curly Joe wondered just where the hell Slocum was going. The direction he was headed would lead eventually to the road between Joshville and Wagon Gap, but then if he took that road in either direction, he would still have ridden several hours longer than necessary. It didn't make any sense. He shrugged and clucked and shook the reins, and the wagon moved forward with a lurch.

Slocum was of two minds. Well, three really. Part of him wanted to just ride along with Curly Joe and the girls and have a hell of a good night in the old line shack. He wondered if Curly Joe and Francine would go ahead and have their fun right in front of Jessie, and her without a man.

Or would Jessie join in on the fun? He hadn't thought of that possibility before. Damn. He realized that he had begun to think of Jessie as his gal, and he told himself that he'd better watch that. He did not want any such entanglements in his life. Hell, he thought, let Curly Joe screw them both.

No matter what was going on back at the shack, there were two other things more pressing in Slocum's mind. One was Waters, the anemic-looking stranger in the black clothes. Slocum was almost certain that the third revolver in the man's belt was his own, the one that had been stolen from him when the freight wagon had been robbed. That meant that the man who was toting it was likely the same man who had hit him from behind. Waters.

Slocum wanted that gun back, and he wanted to even the score with the man who had stolen it from him and scarred the side of his head. And the son of a bitch was back in Joshville, and he seemed to be in cahoots with Gould and his bunch. Slocum thought about riding back into town and finding the bastard, but then that might not be such a good idea.

Even if he did manage to locate Waters, would he be able to deal with him quietly? If not, he might have the whole gang on top of him before he knew it, and then what would he have accomplished? And, of course, he had not gotten a real close look at the gun. There was an outside chance that he was wrong about Waters.

No. Of the three thoughts or impulses in his brain, the one that seemed right, that seemed to make the most sense, was the one he had decided to follow. He was riding back to Bald Knob, the place in the road where he had been ambushed by the five road agents. A wagon had gone out earlier in the day, and if Hogan's new driver was worth his salt, it would be returning just before dark.

If the bandits were planning to hit it again, and if they meant to use their same old pattern, they would be settling into their favorite lurking spot soon, and Slocum wanted to get there first. He wanted time to figure out just where they would hide—all five of them—and then he wanted to find himself a spot where they wouldn't notice him when they came along. That might not be an easy thing to do, and he hoped that he had given himself enough time to do the job right.

There was another reason for going to Bald Knob instead of back to town to look for Waters. If Slocum was right about Waters having been the fifth bandit, then Waters just might be out at Bald Knob again tonight and not in town at all. Bald Knob could wind up taking care of two of Slocum's self-appointed tasks at the same time.

Slocum wanted to even things for himself and for Hogan, and he wanted the gunfighter's wages Hogan would pay him when the job was done. He didn't want to make a career out of the deal, and he was beginning to be tired of the area around Joshville. He wanted to get the job over with and move on to someplace else. Damn near any place.

6

Slocum could see Bald Knob looming before him. He hoped that he was early enough to get there before the bandits. Part of him wanted to hurry on, but a more cautious part told him to take it easy. They could already be in place. He doubted that, for it should be another hour before the wagon would come along. He knew the schedule well, and apparently, so did the outlaws. But the sun was low in the western sky, and schedules were notoriously unreliable in these parts.

He moved on toward Bald Knob slowly, deciding to swing wide around it and come up behind. He knew there was a dry arroyo back there with lots of places to hide his horse. All the long slow way around Bald Knob, Slocum kept his eyes peeled, but he saw nothing to cause concern.

Reaching the arroyo at last, he left the Palouse in a blind draw, took his Winchester, and started to make his way on foot toward the knob. It was a rough climb out of the arroyo and up the back side of the knob, and he was a little winded by the time he reached the top. Still, there was no sign of the outlaws or of the wagon.

He eased himself down into the road and looked back toward Wagon Gap. He could neither see the wagon coming nor hear its clatter. It would either come along on time or late. He had at least another hour, he thought, before the wagon would arrive. He had no way of knowing about the outlaws.

Bald Knob looked like its name from a distance, a large, round boulder sitting atop a hill, but up close it was full of fissures and nestled among numerous smaller rocks. It was a place that could be crawling with all kinds of unseen life: scorpions, lizards, snakes, even two-legged rats and skunks.

Slocum figured out just where he had stopped the wagon, then looked from there for a place where a man could have jumped quickly into the wagon bed from behind him. It didn't take long to discover a small ledge about shoulder high in just the right place. The ledge was in a nook that afforded a good blind. A man in there could not be seen by anyone coming from the direction of Wagon Gap.

Slocum crawled up into the nook and on the ledge to take a look around. He found a few burnt matches and some discarded cigarette butts, the roll-your-own kind, not the newfangled ready-rolls. Someone had been up there and spent some time waiting. He figured that to have been Waters, the man who had jumped into the wagon and hit him from behind, the man who had his Colt.

Still conscious of his timing, Slocum jumped back down into the road. He felt the jar of his landing throughout his body. Damn, he thought, I'm getting too old for this shit. He walked on around the curve in the road to the place where the other four had been waiting. Because of the sharp curve the road took around the knob, there was no need for such a good hiding place there. The four had simply been standing in the road with guns drawn, waiting for the wagon to make the turn.

A quick look around showed evidence of men having waited there against the rock. They probably just lounged around until they heard the wagon's approach, then drew their weapons and spaced themselves across the road. When the surprised driver, busy with the team, came around the curve, he would see them waiting there blocking the road and holding guns on him. He'd be going too slow, because of the grade behind him, to do anything but stop. Then, to make doubly sure, the fifth man would jump down from the nook into the wagon bed.

It was a good plan. It had sure worked on Slocum. But even a good plan can be worked too much. Slocum hoped that the bandits had become cocky with their plan and would try it at least one more time.

He was pretty sure that he knew Waters to be one of them, but he had no real proof. Even if he accused Waters of having stolen his Colt, there could be several different explanations for how the sleazy bastard came by it. He could say that he won it in a card game, or that he found it along the road. Any damn thing.

Slocum wanted to catch them in the act of robbing the wagon, and if both he and the wagon driver could survive the encounter, there would be two witnesses against them. He had to find a spot for himself to wait, and it would have to offer some advantages. He would have to be well hidden, and he would have to be able to swing quickly into action against the outlaws.

He walked around the knob until he found the likeliest-looking place for a climb, and then he went up to the top. He was planning to look around some, but then he heard the sound of horses' hooves approaching. He dropped down flat on top of the knob and looked toward Joshville. Five riders were coming. It had to be the outlaws. He waited, hoping that his silhouette was low enough to avoid detection.

Slocum's heart pounded in his chest, and his palms grew sweaty, as he waited for the riders to reach the knob. At last he got a good look at them, and he recognized them all. Sure enough, they were Waters and the same four Slocum had seen waiting in the road when he had been ambushed. He'd had it figured right. Then, as they drew closer to the knob, he lost sight of them again. He heard them as they stopped their horses and dismounted. He could even hear their voices. He could not see them, and he was afraid that if he stood up to locate a better vantage point, he would give himself away.

Down below, Waters walked around the curve to look toward Wagon Gap. The other four followed him at a leisurely pace.

"No sign of it yet," said Waters. "We got plenty of time."

He reached into his shirt pocket for the makings and rolled himself a smoke. Then he struck a match against the side of the knob and lit his cigarette.

"Just like last time?" asked one of the outlaws.

"Just like always, Sam," said Waters. "Just like always." He drew deep on his cigarette and exhaled a cloud of smoke that quickly dissipated in the wind.

"How many times you think we can pull this same trick before they get wise to it?" Sam asked.

"You getting nervous, Sam?" Waters asked.

"Well, yeah. A little, I guess. It just seems like to me that they'll catch on after so many times. That's all."

"Sam," said Waters, "look down that road. You see anything coming?"

"No."

"Look back the other way then."

Sam walked a few steps back around the curve and looked toward Joshville.

"See anything?" called Waters.

"No. Nothing," said Sam.

"If anything was coming from either direction, you'd see it, wouldn't you?" asked Waters.

"Yeah. I reckon so."

"And you could tell if it was a wagon with just the driver, or if it was a bunch of riders, or if it was a goddamned elephant from a circus, couldn't you?"

"Yeah."

"Then as long as what we see coming along the road is just the wagon with just a driver, we'll keep on doing the same thing we been doing, 'cause it works. If we see a bunch of riders coming along, then we'll change our plans. Now, does that make sense to you?"

"It makes sense to me," said another of the outlaws. "Hell, relax, Sam. We got a pretty good thing going here."

"Yeah, I know," said Sam. "I ain't complaining. It's just that—well, hell, George, it seems too damn easy, I guess, and that makes me nervous."

"Shit," said George, "you'd be nervous in a whore-house."

"Yeah," said another outlaw. "Worrying about it being so damn easy to find yourself a whore."

The outlaws all laughed at that, and even Sam joined

in with a chuckle at his own expense. Waters, however, only smiled, and the smile left his face as quickly as it had appeared there. He took a final drag on his cigarette and flipped the butt over the side of the hill. There was silence for a moment. Then one of the outlaws chuckled. "Nervous in a whorehouse," he said.

"Wagon's coming," said Waters. "Take your places and get quiet. You all know what to do."

Without bothering to watch the others do as he had told them, Waters immediately began scampering up onto the ledge. Once he was up, he scooted back into the nook to hide himself from the approaching wagon driver. He settled back against the rock, making himself comfortable for the wait. He was used to it. He had done it several times before.

The other four went back around the curve in the road and situated themselves in a straight line across the road, thereby blocking the path. Sam nervously drew out his revolver to check its load.

Down the road, the driver was just beginning to fight his team up the steep grade. It took all of his attention, in spite of the fact that he knew he was approaching the dangerous spot where the previous robberies had taken place. He hoped that the bandits would let this wagon through. It seemed like a possibility. It wasn't reasonable to think that they would get away with doing the same thing over and over again. Perhaps this day would be the day they decided to lay low.

Up on top of Bald Knob, Slocum lay flat against the rock. He could see the wagon coming, but it would soon be out of his sight again, for he could not see around the edge of the knob down into the road. He could not see the outlaws, although he was pretty sure he knew where they were. The four would be strung out across the road, right where he had seen them before, and Waters would be in the nook he had found.

That was all well and good, but just what the hell was Slocum going to do about it? He wasn't at all sure that he could even move around on top of the rock without making enough noise to alert the road agents down below. And he didn't even know where he would go. He had not had enough time to locate a spot from which to make his move against the gang. He hadn't even decided from which direction he would attack.

If he came up behind Waters, the four men in the road would be facing him with weapons ready, and the poor driver would be caught in between. If he came up behind the four, Waters would be behind the helpless driver. This was not the way he had planned this maneuver, but then, it had taken so much time for Curly Joe to get the wagon from the ranch, and then for them to get the girls packed and safely onto the Running R, that the day had just gotten away from him.

Well, he thought, that's the way it fell, and I'm here. I'll just have to play it out—one way or another. It would be a damn shame, though, he thought, if all he could do was just lay there on the rock and let the robbery take place right down there below him.

The wagon was still in sight, but it wouldn't be for much longer. He was going to have to make a decision and make it fast. If he delayed much more, the action would start down below and out of his sight, and by then most any move he would make would be a stupid one.

Perhaps, after all, he could stand up and move carefully and quietly along the top of the rock. He couldn't see the outlaws, but then, they couldn't see him either. He decided that he would have to try it.

Slowly and carefully, he eased himself up to his hands and knees. As carefully, he stood. He felt terribly exposed there, standing on top of Bald Knob, even though he knew that the outlaws couldn't see him. He calculated just where the nook might be, and he took a step in that direction.

The footing, which had seemed all right before, suddenly seemed precarious. It would be so easy to kick a loose rock and send it tumbling down the side of the boulder to alert the bandits to danger, or worse yet, to step on one and slip. His steps were slow, almost individual. He stepped and stood still. Then he stepped again. The Winchester was slippery in his damp hands. His heart still pounded in his chest.

He stepped again. He should be moving to a point just above the nook in which Waters was secreted. He thought about the good sense of lying down flat again and just letting happen what was about to happen down below. He thought about it, but he dismissed the thought. There was a wagon driver down below in danger. True, the bandits had not yet killed a driver, but there was always that possibility.

Suppose the driver made a bold but foolish move in an attempt to protect Hogan's money. He would surely be killed. Suppose Waters hit him just a bit too hard. Or suppose even that one of the bandits just got bored with the same routine and decided for the pure fun of it to shoot the man. Any of those things could happen.

And there was his job. He had taken on the responsibility of putting an end to these robberies. He had even made the suggestion to Hogan. At this moment it seemed like a particularly foolish suggestion he had made, but he had made it, and Hogan had agreed, and they had shook hands on the bargain. He had to do whatever he could to protect Hogan's money. He had no other choice.

Finally, there was the matter of his Colt and his pride, and Waters was down there hidden in the same nook from which he had surprised Slocum. That last thought gave Slocum even more determination than had any of the others. Somehow he would get that son of a bitch down there.

He glanced toward the wagon and realized that it was just about to leave his sight lines, and at that moment, for some inexplicable reason, the driver, though he was fighting the team up the steep grade, glanced up. And Slocum could tell that the man had seen him.

7

Well, by God, Slocum wasn't at all sure what it was, but it had happened. Something had started. The driver had no way of knowing who Slocum was or what he was doing up on top of Bald Knob. Slocum himself had insisted on keeping his job with Hogan a secret. But the driver did know that wagons had been robbed there at Bald Knob, and he had just seen a man with a rifle walking on top of the knob itself. What was he to think?

"Whoa! Whoa!" the driver shouted, pulling back on the reins and thoroughly confusing the team. They had been up that grade more often than any one driver, and no one had ever tried to stop them just as they had begun the long hard pull. They neighed and stamped and shook their heads in their confusion. The driver fought them. He set the brake, and he tried to get the animals under control once again, so he could begin to back them down onto the flat, off the grade, into the open, away from the ambush up ahead.

Slocum saw all this, and he decided to take immediate

advantage of the situation. The driver was safe. He would not be caught in the middle. Just to Slocum's left was a place where Bald Knob was round and almost slick. He moved quickly to that spot, sat down, and started to slide. He didn't know exactly where he would land, but he didn't think that it would be smooth all the way to the road.

Down below, Waters, in his nook, had heard the unexpected sounds of confusion and scurrying. "Somebody get out there and see what the hell's going on," he shouted.

Slocum hit a bump hard on his ass. It wasn't quite a ledge, but it was enough of a bump to stop his progress. He was sitting there on the side of the knob, feeling and, he thought, probably looking pretty damn foolish. Just then George and Sam came running around the curve to look for the wagon.

"I knew it," Sam was shouting. "What'd I tell you?"

Both men stopped in the road, six-guns in hand, looking down the grade at the wagon.

"He knows we're here," Sam yelled. "I knew it. I knew it was going to happen."

"Shut up," George snapped.

"What the hell's going on out there?" yelled Waters.

Slocum, from his ridiculous perch, had a perfect view of George and Sam there in the road. He was also in a direct line of sight for the two outlaws, but they had not looked up. They were looking at the wagon down the grade. Slocum raised his rifle and sighted in on George.

"Hold it right there, boys," he called.

The two outlaws looked up to see Slocum sitting on the side of the knob, his rifle aimed in their direction. They stood still a moment, confused. Then George raised his revolver and shouted at the same time.

"Kill him," he said.

Slocum squeezed the trigger and his slug smashed into the chest of George. George's revolver fell unfired into the dirt, and George, dead on his feet, stood wavering for a second or two before falling backward with a thud, sending a puff of dust up from the road and then lying still.

Sam fired a quick shot that kicked up shards of rock just to Slocum's right. Slocum felt bits of rock sting his cheek as he cranked another shell into the chamber of the Winchester, raised it again, and fired again. His shot raked the side of Sam's head, tearing his right ear in half. Blood streamed down the side of Sam's head and neck, soaking his shirt. He dropped his gun, screamed, grabbed his head, and fell to his knees.

Slocum then abandoned all caution and flung himself off the side of the knoll, landing hard in the road, falling forward and rolling. He came to his feet, rifle ready, and looked around. He saw no one except Sam, kneeling and bleeding and holding his head there beside the body of George. He ran forward and tossed Sam's and George's revolvers over the edge of the hill. Then he looked toward the nook. He couldn't see Waters, but he was pretty sure the man was still in there. The other two outlaws were still around the curve and out of sight. He could hear the wagon driver down the grade behind him yelling curses and fighting with the horses.

Unless the other two outlaws decided to come out to fight, Slocum knew that he would have to deal with Waters next. To get after the others, he would have to walk or run right past the nook, and Waters would be able to shoot him in the back. On the other hand, if he tried to mess with Waters, the other two would have a good chance of sneaking around the edge of the knob and taking potshots at him. He was standing out in the middle of the road exposed.

Sam didn't look as if he would cause any more trouble, but Slocum knew that anything could happen. He decided to put Sam totally out of commission so he could forget about him and concentrate on the remaining three. He stepped in close and smashed Sam on top of the head with the butt of his Winchester, knocking him cold, putting him, at least for the moment, out of his misery and out of the picture. Then he started walking toward the nook.

He was close enough to be able to see a little ways into the nook, but Waters must have been all the way back, for he couldn't see him. He glanced ahead and saw no one peering around the curve. He raised his Winchester and fired three quick shots into the nook. There was no way he could get a direct hit, but the ricochets might annoy the bastard. Then he ran over to hug the wall of the knob and waited. He felt the sweat running down his forehead, and he wiped it with a sleeve to keep it out of his eyes. The silence at Bald Knob was broken only by the sounds of the wagon and team at the bottom of the grade.

Ernest Middleton, the driver, had finally gotten the wagon back down on level ground, and he was talking to the team, trying to settle them down. He glanced up toward Bald Knob to make sure that none of the action up there was headed down his way. The shooting had ceased, at least for the moment. He couldn't tell what, if anything, was happening. He grabbed a rifle from under the seat and jumped down out of the wagon.

He moved to the left side of the wagon and, holding his rifle ready, watched the rise. He could make out one man pressed against the knob. It looked as if the fight wasn't over. He wondered who was up there fighting. He had seen one man on top of the knob earlier and had assumed that it was one of the bandits.

Thinking that it was likely that he was about to be ambushed, he had stopped the team and backed them down the grade. Then someone had started shooting up there. He had thought at first that they were shooting at him, but then it had become obvious that they were not. There were men up there shooting at one another. Had someone come along to prevent the planned holdup? He hoped so.

Slocum was getting tired of waiting. The two outlaws around the curve could be making their escape, abandoning Waters to his fate. He wanted some action, but he didn't want to make any fool moves.

"Come on out of there, you chicken shit," he called.

A shout from the nook answered him. "Come and get me."

Slocum waited another tense moment. Then the voice from the nook shouted again.

"Orvel! Merv! What the hell's going on out there? Get that son of a bitch so I can get out of here."

Suddenly a gunman came running around the curve with a revolver in each hand. He saw Slocum and started shooting wild. Bullets hit the side of the knob all around Slocum as he raised his rifle and took careful aim. He squeezed the trigger, and hot lead tore through the outlaw's right shoulder, causing him to spin to the right. He screamed and cursed. He stopped spinning, facing Slocum once again, and he raised the gun in his left hand. Slocum cranked another bullet into the chamber and raised the Winchester.

"Don't try it," he warned.

The outlaw hesitated, then thumbed back the hammer

on his revolver. Slocum fired into the man's chest. The outlaw jerked and staggered forward a couple of steps before his knees buckled. He looked at Slocum with wide eyes, his mouth hanging open. His fingers went limp, and the gun dropped from his hand. Then he fell forward, landing hard on his face, but he didn't feel it. He was dead.

There was still one more around the curve, and Slocum didn't want any of them getting away, not if he could help it. The odds were a whole lot better now, and he decided on a bold move. He edged himself closer to the nook, took a deep breath, then started to run.

As he ran, he fired into the nook, one shot after another. That should keep Waters huddled well to the back of the nook and therefore out of the fight. Nearing the curve, Slocum forgot about Waters and looked ahead. He ran around the curve ready to shoot, but no one was there. He looked up and around in a moment of panic. The man might be hidden behind a rock, maybe up above somewhere.

Then he heard rapid footsteps and looked down the road toward Joshville. The man had run for the horses. Slocum took aim, but it was a long shot. The man climbed onto the back of a horse, and the other four horses scattered as he lashed at his mount, riding hard for town.

Slocum started to try a shot, then changed his mind and lowered the rifle. He would probably have missed and wasted a bullet, for it would have been a long shot at a moving target. Besides, it might be best after all to let one of them get away. He knew that he would recognize the man if he ever saw him again, and it might prove to be very interesting to see where the man went, to whom he would run.

Slocum's mind raced back to Waters in the nook. He'd had ample time to get down and be coming up behind Slocum. Slocum turned quickly, but he saw no one. He started walking back around the curve. Waters was alone now, wherever he was. And to make his escape he had to go past either Slocum or the wagon driver. There was no other way. Not unless he wanted to try to climb the steep face of Bald Knob.

Slocum rounded the curve and still saw no one. He walked up near the nook and held the Winchester ready.

"Waters," he said. "Waters. I know who you are, and I know you're in there. Toss out your guns and then show yourself."

He waited, but there was no response.

"This is my last warning," Slocum said. "Toss out your guns or I start shooting."

Still there was no response, and Slocum fired six shots into the nook. He waited for the smoke and the dust to clear, and still he had heard nothing from inside the nook. He moved up to the wall and started to climb.

It was a short but nervous climb. It felt like poking one's nose into a rattler's den. It felt foolish, but the alternative was to stand out in the road shouting, maybe only to the rocks. Waters might have managed to slip out somehow, and Slocum could be shooting at and talking to nothing.

Slowly he poked his head above the ledge. He saw no one, but then, it looked darker in there than he remembered it from before. He moved up a little further. No one jumped him. No one shot at him. He drew a knee up onto the ledge and pulled himself on up. He stopped in a crouch, rifle ready. Then he saw the body.

Waters was curled up on the ledge at the back of the nook like a child asleep. The body was covered with blood. Damn, thought Slocum. It looks like almost every one of those damn ricochets had hit him someplace.

He took hold of the shirt collar and dragged the body out toward the rim of the ledge. When he had it stretched out on its back and had a little more maneuvering room for himself, he reached down and pulled the Colt revolver out of the belt. It was his all right. Since he wasn't wearing his empty holster, he tucked the Colt into his own waistband. Then he shoved Waters's body on over the edge and let it fall to the road.

He dropped back down into the road himself and walked toward the wagon a few steps. He could see that the driver had taken cover behind the wagon and was holding a rifle ready. He waved an arm over his head.

"Is that you, Ernie?" he called.

His answer was another question. "Who the hell wants to know?"

"It's John Slocum, Ernie," Slocum yelled. "Come on up. The fight's over."

"Slocum?" said Ernie. "Hell. How do I know you ain't one of them? The way you and Hogan been cussing each other, I ain't sure about you. What happened up there anyhow?"

"There was five men up here, Ernie," Slocum called. "The same ones that robbed me. I killed three of them. One run off, and one's up here hurt. Come on up."

"Hell, no," Ernie said. "I ain't going up there. If you're telling me the truth, put down your guns and walk down here to me."

8

"Aw shit, Ernie," said Slocum, and he walked over to the edge of the knob again to lean his Winchester against the wall. He reluctantly pulled the rescued Colt out of his trousers and laid it gingerly on a flat rock. Then he held up his hands and started walking down the grade toward the wagon.

"Ernie, damn it, I ain't one of the bandits," he said.

"How do I know?" said Ernie. "Just keep coming easy. I'd hate to shoot you down, Slocum. I ain't never had nothing against you."

Slocum moved on down to the bottom of the grade. He started to lower his hands, but Ernie barked at him and poked his rifle barrel into the air in Slocum's direction.

"Just keep them up," he said. "I ain't letting you catch me off guard. No, sir."

"Ernie, there was five men up there on top waiting to ambush you," said Slocum. "Just the same as they did me. Just the same. Four of them was strung across the road just around the curve. The fifth one was hiding in a little nook up on the side of the rock. He's the one that jumped down into the back of the wagon and hit me from behind.''

"There might have been five, and there might have been six," said Ernie.

"Then what the hell was the shooting all about?" said Slocum, exasperated. "The bastards were trying to kill me.''

"Maybe they was and maybe they warn't," said Ernie. "All I know is that I heard shots. I don't know who was shooting at who. You might be trying to draw me into a trap."

"The trap was laid, you dumb bastard. I broke it up.''

"That's what you say. Even if you was fighting them, ain't you ever heard of a falling out amongst thieves? I sure have.''

"All right, Ernie," said Slocum. "Listen to me. That fight between me and Hogan—that was all a fake. It was just to throw the road agents off guard. Hogan never fired me. I'm still working for him, and my job was to stop these holdups. That's why I was here."

"Ha, ha," said Ernie. "You think I'm stupid? I heard you two cussing each other, and that was for real. There warn't no fake about it. I was there, and I heard you.''

"Well, look," said Slocum, at last resigned to the fact that Ernie was immovable, "you can see that I ain't armed no more. Can I at least put my hands down?''

"Go ahead," said Ernie, "but don't make no sudden moves. This thing'll put a great big hole right through your middle parts.''

Slowly Slocum lowered his hands. He leaned on the wagon just across from Ernie and lowered his head. He was tired, and the situation with Ernie wasn't helping things at all.

"Now Ernie," he said, "suppose I get up there and drive the wagon, and you sit back in the box with your gun at my back. Will you feel safe enough about that?"

Ernie wasn't sure, but he couldn't think of any alternative other than staying just as they were or shooting Slocum down in cold blood. He didn't like either of those choices.

"Climb on up," he said.

Slocum drove to the top of the grade and stopped the team. He set the brake. The body of Waters was in the road just behind them and that of George was up ahead a little ways. Beside George's body, Sam was stirring and moaning. A third body was lying in the road a little farther along. Ernie gave a low whistle and shoved the hat back on his head.

"Boy, oh, boy," he said. "You did have a fight up here."

He put the rifle down in the wagon bed and jumped out the back end to stand in the road.

"What do we do now?" he asked.

Slocum breathed a sigh of relief that the rifle was no longer pointed at his back. He turned on the seat to face Ernie.

"My guns are over there against the rock," he said, pointing. "I'd like to load them up and load up these bodies and that one wounded fellow over there and drive on back into Joshville. Get the horses too, including my own."

He sat still, waiting for a response from Ernie. Ernie thought for a moment, then walked over to the wall of the knob and picked up Slocum's Colt and Winchester. He turned to face Slocum and check his reaction. Slocum had not moved. Ernie walked to the wagon and handed the weapons up to Slocum.

"Hell, Slocum," he said, "I reckon you ain't lying to me."

Slocum took his weapons, laid them on the wagon seat, then jumped down into the road. He and Ernie together loaded the three bodies into the back of the wagon. Then they each grabbed Sam by an arm and pulled him to his feet. He yelled like he was being tortured.

"Be careful," Sam said. "I'm shot bad. I'm like to die."

"Not from that shot," said Slocum. "All it did was tear your ear. Come on."

They made him ride in the back of the wagon with the bodies of his buddies. Then they collected the horses and drove on into Joshville. It was late when they pulled up in front of Hogan's office. The sun was low in the western sky. People came out of the saloons to see what had happened, and Hogan came out of the office. He looked at what was left of the outlaws in the bed of his wagon, and he smiled.

"By God, John," he said, "that didn't take long."

"I guess you are still working for Mr. Hogan after all," said Ernie. He climbed down out of the wagon and handed Hogan a small bag. Hogan hefted the bag for weight in his right palm and smiled.

"I guess the secret's out now, Slocum," said Hogan.

"Yeah," Slocum answered.

"Come on inside. Ernie, why don't you run and find Brady for us?" Hogan said. Then he turned and went back into the office. Slocum jumped out of the wagon and followed.

"What happened?" Hogan asked as soon as the door had been shut behind Slocum.

"Pretty much just what I planned," said Slocum. "I got there before they did. I got clean up on top of Bald Knob, so when they showed, they didn't know I was there. They hid themselves just the way they did before. When I saw Ernie coming, I showed myself up on top. Course, he didn't know who I was. All he knew was that someone was up there at the ambush spot, and he hauled up down at the bottom of the grade. That left just me and the outlaws, and as you saw out there, I got four of them. One of them's still alive."

"I see you got your Colt back too," said Hogan.

Slocum smiled. "Yeah," he said. "Three of them out there, including the live one, were among the four that I said I'd be able to recognize. Them and the one that got away were the four standing in the road. The other one out there, the one dressed in black, must have been the one who jumped me from behind. He had my Colt, and he was hid in a place where he could jump down in the wagon bed like that."

"Goddamn, Slocum," said Hogan, slapping a hand on the money bag, which he had placed there on his desk. "It sure feels good. I'd say you've earned a bonus."

"I ain't so sure about that," said Slocum. "I don't think the job's finished yet."

"What do you mean?"

Just then Brady came into the office. His face was red, and he was puffing, but he also seemed to be visibly shaken about something. Slocum wondered how long it had been since the man had seen a dead outlaw. Or could it be something else?

"What the hell's happened?" Brady demanded.

"Slocum here jumped the outlaws that jumped him—and my other drivers," said Hogan. "He got them—all but one."

"And I'll know him when I see him again," said Slocum.

"How do we know them's the outlaws out there?" Brady asked.

"Who the hell else would they be?" said Hogan.

"I recognized four of them from when they held me up," said Slocum.

"I told you if you ever seen them again to come and tell me," said Brady. "Not to just up and kill them. There'll have to be a hearing on this."

"I didn't have time to come after you, Brady," Slocum said. "They were laying in wait for the wagon, just like before, in the exact same spot, and the wagon was on its way up the grade."

"You said you recognized four of them," said Brady. "What about the fifth one?"

"He was with them," said Slocum, "and he had my Colt."

"One Colt revolver looks pretty much like another," said Brady.

"I know my Colt."

"Marshal," said Hogan, "why don't you stop questioning Slocum and go lock up that outlaw that's sitting out there in the wagon?"

"Don't be telling me how to do my job, Hogan," said Brady.

"Someone needs to," Hogan said.

Brady chose to ignore Hogan's last remark and turned on Slocum once again. "Don't you be leaving town," he said. "This business ain't done with yet."

"I'll be around," said Slocum.

"I'd better get that fellow out there over to the jail," Brady said, as if the idea had just occurred to him. "He looks like he might need a doctor too. And I'll have to find Paul to take charge of the bodies. Damn it, Slocum, you can sure cause a hell of a lot of trouble for only just one man."

Brady huffed his way out of the office, slamming the door behind himself. Hogan looked at Slocum.

"You'd think the worthless bastard would appreciate what you've done," he said. "Hell, you've gone and done his job for him."

"I've got a thought about that," said Slocum, "but it's nothing I can prove. Not yet."

"Tell me about it."

"Well, let's start with his honor your mayor," Slocum said.

"Gould? What about him? He's a cheap politician."

"I don't know about politics," said Slocum, "but think about this. Gould keeps a bunch of hardcases around him all the time. I seen Waters with them yesterday. He's the one out there in black, the one that had my Colt."

"You think that Gould is mixed up in these robberies?" Hogan asked.

"Is the marshal elected or appointed?" said Slocum, ignoring Hogan's question.

"Well, he's appointed."

"Who appoints him?"

"The mayor."

"Right now, Toby Reed's running for office against Gould," said Slocum. "Right?"

"That's right."

"Gould set his men on me just because he seen me and one of Reed's hands having a drink together. That seems like more than just politics to me. A politician will cuss his opponent and maybe even tell lies on him, but when he starts beating up on folks, it seems to me like he's desperate to hold onto that office for some reason that he ain't telling.''

Hogan was sitting on the front edge of his desk rubbing his chin in deep thought. He stood up and paced across the room, then turned to face Slocum again.

"I think maybe you've got something there," he said. "Gould's got things pretty much his own way here in Joshville. He pretty much runs the town, and he gets his way much of the time by bullying folks. I guess I've kind of ignored it because he's never tried bullying me.''

"At least not out in the open," Slocum said.

"Yeah," said Hogan, glancing down at his money bag. "I see what you mean. You know, he did once offer to buy me out. I turned him down.''

"What would happen if these robberies continued?" Slocum asked.

"I told you before," said Hogan. "I'd have been forced out of business.''

"And Gould could have bought you out cheap.''

"Yeah. Or just waited for me pack up and leave and then take over. Damn it, John, I think you're right about this.''

"Well, take it easy, Boss," said Slocum. "We can't say anything until we get some kind of proof.''

"I don't suppose you've got any ideas about how we're going to do that," Hogan said.

Slocum took a cigar out of his pocket, and Hogan struck a match on his desk top and offered it. Slocum puffed to get his smoke going, then backed off.

"Thanks," he said. "Well, I ain't exactly got any

ideas about that, but I do think that maybe you and me ought to go out to the Running R and talk all this over with old Toby Reed. Seems to me like we've all got the same goal in mind. What do you think?''

9

Brady picked up the slightly wounded Sam from the back of the wagon and led him off to the jail, where his torn ear was tended to by the local doctor. The only damage done to his head by Slocum's rifle butt was a goose-egg knot. Meanwhile, Slocum mounted his big Palouse and rode out of town headed back toward the Running R. Through a window from the White Horse, Harrison Gould watched all of these occurrences with keen interest. Close behind him, Red and Smitty hovered. Smitty still wore cotton in his ears.

"Red," said Gould, "get over to the jailhouse and find out what's going on. Tell Brady to get his ass over here and see me."

Red hurried out the front door, and Gould took a seat at a table near the window.

"What do you want me to do, Boss?" said Smitty.

"Go get me a bottle and a glass," said Gould.

"Sure," said Smitty. He took two steps, stopped, and turned back. "Two glasses?"

"Get four."

"Four? Okay."

As soon as Smitty returned from the bar, Gould poured himself a drink. Smitty took the bottle and poured one for himself. Gould tossed his down with one gulp and refilled the glass.

"Something went wrong," he said. "Something somewhere went bad wrong."

"Waters must have really screwed up this time, huh?" said Smitty.

"Shut up," said Gould. "Run over there and take a look at them bodies in the wagon. Hurry it up."

Smitty tossed down his drink, scooted back his chair, and hustled to the door and out. Gould polished off his second drink and poured himself a third. Things were suddenly falling apart around him. He couldn't allow that to happen. He had control of Joshville, and he wanted to keep it that way. It had been a very profitable business, one that he had no intention of ending. He took a sip from his third glass of whiskey, and Smitty came scurrying back into the White Horse and over to the table. He resumed his seat.

"It's Waters and them all right," he said. "Deader'n hell. Waters and George and Orvel. Course old Sam got took off to jail. Ain't no sign of Merv. But them others is deader'n hell. Old Waters, he don't look so damn tough now."

"Shit," said Gould. "It's that goddamned Slocum. I should have had him killed instead of just beat up. Hell, you assholes didn't even do a good job of beating him up. Did you?"

Smitty's face took on a serious pout, and he noticed the ringing in his ears get louder. Just then Red came back inside followed by Brady. They walked over to the table where Gould and Smitty waited, pulled out chairs for themselves, and sat down. Gould shoved the bottle toward them.

"Help yourselves," he said. "Brady, what the hell's going on?"

"That Slocum wiped out your road agents," said Brady.

"By his lonesome?"

"It looks like it. He killed them all but Sam and maybe Merv. Shot Sam's ear in half and conked him on the head. There ain't no sign of Merv. No telling if he's out there dead or if he got away. Slocum says he got away."

"Then why the hell didn't he come in here to tell me what happened?" said Gould.

Brady shrugged.

"Maybe he's laying low," said Red.

"Or maybe he just lit out," Smitty added.

"Ain't no telling," said Brady. "Anyhow, I got Sam over in the jail. It's the only thing I could do. Seems like Hogan never really did fire Slocum. Just kind of pretended to so Slocum could catch the outlaws."

"He did too," said Smitty. "All by his lonesome."

"Any way we can get Slocum for murder?" Gould asked. "Say that them wasn't the outlaws?"

"I already tried that," said Brady. "I kind of hinted that we didn't know for sure, but then, like I said, Hogan had Slocum hired just to get the outlaws. Seems Slocum hid out up there at Bald Knob and waited for them to lay their ambush. When the wagon come along, that's when the shooting started."

"So the driver was there too," said Gould.

"Yeah," said Brady. "They got Slocum's word and the driver's. It was old Ernie. Then, of course, they also

got the word of Hogan that Slocum was working for
him just for that purpose. Slocum said too that he recognized them all except Waters from when they held
him up.''

"So they got a pretty good case if it goes to court,"
said Gould.

"I think so," the marshal agreed.

"Well, it can't go to court," said Gould. "See to it."

"Well, what about Sam?" asked Brady.

"You heard me," said Gould. "See to it. And get out
there and find Merv."

He stood up and stalked away, leaving the other three
men sitting at the table with the whiskey. Brady poured
himself another drink.

"Sam's in the first cell," he said. "No one else is
over there. The front door's unlocked."

Smitty and Red looked at one another, and Brady
lifted his glass to drink. Red shoved back his chair.

"Come on, Smitty," he said.

"Boys," said Brady, "be careful. And be quiet."

Smitty and Red looked up and down the street to make
sure no one was watching. Then they slipped quickly
and quietly into the marshal's office. Standing just inside
the dark room, they looked around again.

"Brady?" came Sam's voice from the cell. "Brady,
that you?"

"Be quiet, Sam," said Red. "It ain't Brady."

"Who is it?"

"It's Red and Smitty. Keep quiet."

Red moved across the room to the nearest cell, where
he found Sam clutching the bars and straining to see out
into the darkness.

"Red?" he said. "Smitty? You come to get me out of here?"

"Yeah," said Red, "so keep your voice down. We don't want to attract no attention. Smitty, find the keys."

"How come Brady didn't let me out of here?" Sam asked.

"He had to make it look good," said Red. "There was too many people watching. Just take it easy. We'll have you out of here in a minute."

"I can't find the goddamn keys," said Smitty.

"Brady hangs them right there on the wall," Red said.

"Well, they ain't here."

"Oh, hell."

Red moved over to where Smitty was squinting and feeling around on the wall. He looked at the pegs on the wall and found them all empty.

"Hurry up and do something," Sam whined. "I want out of here, and Gould promised us that we'd be protected. I don't know why Brady even put me in here in the first place."

"Just calm down," said Red. "The keys got to be here someplace."

He moved over to Brady's desk and rummaged through some papers. At last he found the keys where a poster had fallen on top of them.

"Here they are," he said. "See? Now we'll get you right out of there. Here, Smitty. Open the door."

Red handed the keys to Smitty, and while Smitty stepped up to the cell door to insert the key in the lock, Red stepped up close to the bars just to the right of the door. He leaned his back against the bars, and his right hand went to the handle of a long knife at his belt.

Smitty was fumbling with the keys, trying to find the right one for the lock.

"Hurry up," said Sam. His attention was all on Smitty's hands and the keys. Red slowly slid the knife out of its sheath. Smitty fit a key into the lock and turned it. It worked.

"There," he said. He pulled open the cell door, and Sam stepped out, but just as he did, Red slid the long blade into his back. Sam sucked in air. His mouth fell open, and his eyes were wide. He stiffened.

"You shit," he said.

Red jerked his knife free and stepped back as Sam crumpled in the open doorway of the cell.

"Is he dead?" asked Smitty.

Red knelt beside the body and leaned over close. Then he wiped his knife blade clean on Sam's shirt and stood up, slipping the knife back into the sheath. He looked Smitty in the eyes.

"He's dead," he said. "Let's go."

Gould was alone in his office across the street from the White Horse. He watched out a window as Red and Smitty came skulking out of the marshal's office, and he assumed, by their manner, that they had done their job. They better have, the dumb shits, he said to himself. He poured himself a whiskey and sat down heavily in his big overstuffed chair behind the desk.

Where the hell, he wondered, was Merv? Of all the road agents in his employ, only Merv was left alive— that is, if Red and Smitty had done their job over at the jailhouse.

He was worried about Merv. He had no trust in the man: a second-rate gunslinger who needed someone strong to lead him along every step of he way and to bolster his courage. That had been Waters's role, but with Waters dead, Merv was a definite liability. He might blab to anyone in order to save his own hide, or he might blab just to be blabbing.

At daylight, Gould decided, he would send Red out to locate and get rid of Merv once and for all. Then there would be no one left to connect him with the freight wagon robberies. He chided himself mildly for having allowed the last one, the disastrous one, to take place. He should have waited a bit, but he was anxious to break Hogan's back and take over the freight business. The extra bucks in his safe were nice to have too.

How the hell could he have known that Slocum was still working secretly for Hogan? That bastard Slocum had caused all of his problems. He should have had Red kill Slocum that first time he saw the man having a drink with that damned cowboy from the Running R.

There had to be a connection between Slocum and Reed, the man who wanted so badly to unseat him and take over his position as mayor of Joshville. Gould told himself that he couldn't let that happen. He wouldn't. He'd have Merv killed and Slocum too. Reed too if he had too. No one was going to ruin the setup he had there in Joshville. No one.

Merv lurked alone in the arroyos beneath Bald Knob. There was nowhere else to hide. He had started toward Joshville, but before he had ridden halfway, he'd changed his mind. Whoever that damned gunfighter was, he might be riding on into town with the wagon. So Merv had doubled back toward the knob and ridden down into the arroyo. There were lots of twists and turns, and a man ought to be able to hide out in there damn near forever—if he had to.

He had thought about riding to Wagon Gap, but it was a long ride for a man alone who was being hunted, and he was sure that he was being hunted. He was being hunted by that damn driver they had robbed the last time, the same one who had come back and laid an ambush for their ambush.

He had once heard someone in the gang say that the man was a notorious gunman, and someone else had said, "Then why ain't I heard about him?" That had been the end of the discussion, but Merv was thinking, now that he was hiding in the dry arroyo, that the discussion should have continued. They should have made it a point to find out just who this mysterious gunfighter, posing as a humble driver of freight, really was.

Merv wasn't sure, but he thought that he was likely the only survivor of the gang. If anyone else had survived, he wondered where they might be. He would have to find his way into Joshville, probably under cover of dark, and ask Gould to protect him, to tell him what to do and where to go. He thought again about riding toward Wagon Gap and then to places further west, but he didn't have enough money to allow him to feel comfortable with that plan. Maybe Gould would give him a final payoff and finance his flight. And the sooner the better, for he was hungry and thirsty. If only he could manage to find his way to Gould without the gunfighter finding him first.

10

Slocum found his way easily back to the spot where he had ridden away from Curly Joe and the two women. He could see Titty Hill, and Curly Joe had said that the shack was just on the other side of the hill. It was dark, but he gave the Palouse its head. He didn't feel safe or comfortable in Joshville, and besides, there was good company waiting for him at the line shack.

He found the shack dark, and there was no sign of any horses around. Curly Joe did have a job. Perhaps he had to get back to the ranch headquarters with the wagon and team and then be ready for work in the morning. If so, the women would be inside alone. Unless the shack was indeed abandoned, as it appeared to be. Unless something had gone wrong. Could some of Gould's men have gotten bold or desperate enough to invade the Running R after all?

He rode on in close and watched the cabin for a moment. He checked the Colt at his side and found it very comforting. He realized that he normally took it for granted. Having been without it for a while, though, he surely did appreciate it. There was no light in the cabin, no sounds. He couldn't just sit there all night. He had to do something.

"Jessie!" he called out. "Francine! You all in there?"

"Is that you, John?"

He recognized Jessie's voice, and he rode up closer to the door feeling a tremendous sense of relief.

"It's me," he said. "You all right?"

Jessie pulled the door open and looked out at Slocum. Even in the darkness, he thought that he could read the relief in the expression on her face.

"We're fine, John," she said, "but we're sure glad to see you."

"Just give me a minute to take care of my horse," he said, "and I'll be right in."

Jessie stood in the doorway watching as Slocum took his horse to the small corral nearby, unsaddled him, and let him drink at the trough. He looked around and found some oats to feed the big stallion. Then he walked on over to the door of the cabin. He found Francine standing close behind Jessie.

"I guess," he said, "that ole Curly Joe had to get back to the ranch headquarters."

"That's what he said," said Francine.

"He said that old Reed had been mad enough at just bringing us all out here," said Jessie. "The only reason he went along was that we're all in trouble because of Gould. Curly Joe didn't want to push his luck with his boss by staying out here for the night."

"Well," said Slocum, "that makes sense, I guess. Do we have to sit in the dark in here?"

"Not anymore," said Jessie. "In here by ourselves, we felt better that way."

She lit a lantern on the table, and Slocum took a look around the shack. It was remarkably neat and clean for a line shack on a big cattle ranch, and it was well furnished. It had everything anyone would need: table and chairs, cookstove, a couple of beds.

"Want a drink?" Jessie asked.

"Thanks," said Slocum, and Jessie got the bottle and a glass and poured him some whiskey. He pulled out a chair and sat down at the table. Taking the glass from Jessie, he took a healthy sip and enjoyed the feeling of the liquor burning its way down his throat. Jessie took a chair and sat beside him.

"We're sure glad you're back," she said. "I know Curly Joe said we'd be safe here, that Gould and his men are afraid to come onto the Running R. Even so, I have to admit that we were just a bit nervous out here at night by ourselves."

"I reckon so," said Slocum. He took a cigar out of his pocket. Jessie got up and found a match on a nearby shelf.

"Yeah," said Francine. "Where the hell did you go that was so damned important anyhow?"

Jessie struck the match and held it in cupped hands so that Slocum could light his smoke. He took his time puffing, and at last smoke billowed around his head in thick clouds.

"Well," he said, "I just went to wipe out a gang of highway robbers. That's all."

"I'm sure," said Francine.

"I did," said Slocum. "There was five of them. One got away. One went to jail with just his ear shot. The other three are dead."

"Who were they?" Jessie asked.

"Remember that Waters fellow?"

"Yeah."

"He was their leader. The others I recognized from the day they robbed me. That was the only time I'd ever seen them until tonight."

He finished his whiskey and stood up to unbuckle his gunbelt.

"It's been a long day," said Jessie. "You ready for bed?"

Slocum glanced over at the beds.

"It looks inviting," he said.

"You ready to go to sleep?" Jessie said, her arms encircling his neck.

"Well, now," said Slocum, "that all depends."

He took a final puff on his cigar and laid it aside in an ashtray there on the table. Jessie started toying with the front of his shirt.

"It might be more convenient," said Francine, "if we was to shove these two beds together."

Jessie pulled Slocum's head to hers and kissed him full on the lips. Reluctantly, Slocum pulled away from her.

"I reckon I can manage that," he said, and he dragged one bed over until it was snug against the other. When he straightened up and turned to face Jessie, he found both women standing there close. Francine gave him a gentle push backward, and he sat down on the edge of the bed. Jessie knelt to pull off his boots, and while she was thus engaged, Francine began to strip there in front of him.

As he watched the lovely breasts of Francine burst forth, he recalled what he had imagined earlier about Curly Joe being alone with the two women. Things had turned out just the opposite. He wondered what thoughts were running through Curly Joe's mind just at this precise moment.

Jessie pulled his jeans off and tossed them aside, and Francine was wriggling out of her long, full skirt. Slocum couldn't help but marvel at her shapely legs and hips. Then he was naked and so was Francine, and Jessie stood up to strip. Slocum sat on the edge of the bed as Francine moved toward him. She stepped in close, standing between his knees, and he reached his arms around her slim waist.

She moved in even closer and held his head with both her hands, pressing it tight against her just between her ample breasts. Slocum slid his hands around until he gripped one in each, and Francine moaned with pleasure and moved her knees up to the bed, one on each side of Slocum. She was straddling his lap. He felt his cock swelling. Over her shoulder, he could see that Jessie was now naked.

Francine reached down to grip Slocum's cock, and it reacted appropriately, standing stiff and hard, and she guided it to the entrance of her wet cunt, then settled down slowly on it, taking its full length into her depths.

There wasn't much humping Slocum could do in that position, so he just held on to her as she began to rock her hips back and forth and moan happily. Jessie knelt on the bed beside them and put her arms around them both, and Slocum felt her tongue in his ear. In a moment, though, she quit doing that.

"Come on, honey," she said to Francine. "Share some of that with me."

With a groan, Francine backed off, and Slocum moved around until he was lying out flat on the bed. Jessie bent over him and took the wet cock into her mouth, sucking and slurping until all traces of Francine's juices were gone. Then she mounted it and rode it hard. Francine, on her hands and knees, leaned over Slocum's face and kissed his mouth. Their tongues dueled, and he fondled her heavy tits. Then she moved so that one of the marvels was right there in front of his face, and he took it in his mouth and sucked and licked at the nipple. Down below, Jessie still rocked on his rod.

Then Jessie roared out her sudden pleasure and release, and Slocum could feel the cunt juices spreading as they ran free and mixed with the sweat that already coated both his and Jessie's crotches. Jessie shivered violently, then relaxed and fell forward, leaning against Francine's back.

"My turn?" asked Francine.

Jessie backed off of Slocum's still-hard cock and rolled over on her back beside him. Francine started to move, but Slocum stopped her.

"Stay right where you are," he said, and he moved around behind her on his knees and drove his rod into her cunt from behind.

"Oh. Oh," she shouted. "Give it to me, honey."

He withdrew almost to the point of slipping out, then rammed it home again, and as he did, his full ball sack swung against her. He drove again and again, and Jessie, lying there beside them, listened to the sounds of his flesh slapping Francine's, and she thought that he looked like a big powerful bull servicing a cow.

Slocum kept driving in and out, and he noticed that Jessie raised herself up and started to move, but he didn't pay much attention to that. He was too occupied with slamming into Francine's cunt and slapping himself into the pretty round ass there in front of him. He forgot all about Jessie, until he felt her hands creep down his ass and begin to tickle his balls. He drove harder and faster into Francine, and Jessie gripped his sack with one hand, squeezing his balls, not hard enough to hurt, just enough to heighten his sensations.

But the fooling with his balls had another effect. Even though she had just experienced a marvelous climax, Jessie felt herself getting horny for more. She got down on her hands and knees just beside Francine, pressed right up against her, and the two women looked at one another and smiled.

"Hey," Jessie said, "over here, John."

Slocum drove hard once more into Francine, then pulled out and moved behind Jessie. She reached back between her own legs with one hand to guide Slocum's cock into just the right spot. Then he drove hard into her still-wet cunt, all the way.

"Ah," she cried.

"Screw her, baby," said Francine. "Screw her like you screwed me. Hard and fast."

Slocum didn't need the encouragement. He was already driving hard and fast, slamming into Jessie's firm, round ass, pumping deep, in and out of her squishy cunt. He felt the pressure building deep inside himself, and knew that the release would come soon in great gushes.

He pulled out again and moved once more behind Francine, not waiting for her guiding hand. He drove into her all at once, causing her to cry out in surprise. She wiggled her ass in pleasure as he thrust into her, trying with each stab to go even deeper than the last, shaking her entire body with each new and near-violent plunge. Sweat ran down Francine's breasts and droplets fell from the nipples onto the bedsheet below.

"Ohhh," she cried. "I'm coming."

Slocum decided that was as good a time as any for

him to finish, and he rammed once more into her and relaxed, letting it come. The first spurt went deep into her dark and damp tunnel. He pulled out quickly, and the second shot creamed her ass. He moved over behind Jessie, and a third round splashed against her spine and started to run down the crack of her ass. Then he shoved his cock into her cunt to finish. He fired three more times, and then he was done.

He stayed there, on his knees, one hand on each of her ass cheeks, relaxing from the effort, luxuriating in the marvelous sensation, and feeling puffed up and proud from having just satisfied two women with the same long screw.

He felt his cock growing soft and limp inside her, and he let it take its own time slipping loose and flopping down between his legs. It was wet against his ball sack. It was wet with the thick, sweet juices of two beautiful women. Gently he parted Francine and Jessie just enough to turn around and lie down on his back between them.

"It's been a long day," he said, "and I've had it, ladies, but it sure was wonderful."

Francine looked over at Jessie as she took hold of Slocum's limp dick and felt the juices, now beginning to dry to a stickiness. She smiled.

"Shall we clean him up?" she asked.

Jessie returned the smile. "I think he deserves it," she said.

Then the two women put their heads together over his crotch, and they began licking and sucking in turns, cleaning his cock and balls and crotch area the way a mother cat cleans her young.

11

Harrison Gould was frightened. He had thought that he had everything under control, that he owned Joshville and everything in it. Perhaps not literally, at least not yet, but figuratively for sure. For a long time now he had had things his own way—mostly. He wanted Hogan's freight business, and Hogan had thus far refused to sell. But that had been all right, because Gould's gang of road agents had been stealing all of Hogan's profits. That had made it almost as much fun as getting the company, and if things had continued that way, he would have wound up with the company sooner or later anyhow.

Of course, there had been Reed, but Reed had never been a real problem, not until recently, when he had decided to run against Gould for mayor. What the hell did Reed want anyway? Did he want to take over the town? Steal it away from Gould? Gould couldn't think of any other possible reason for Reed's sudden turn.

Gould, who never did anything except for personal

profit, couldn't conceive of anyone else ever having any other reason for doing anything.

Well, whatever reasons Reed might have, he had to be stopped. The setup had been too good for Gould there in Joshville for him to just let go of it when the going got tough. And he could think of three reasons it had gotten tough. The first was Hogan's stubbornness, and he'd have been able to handle that.

Then there was Reed's opposition. He thought that he could handle that too, although Reed was powerful. Gould had never had the guts to attack Reed out on the Running R, but then, Reed had never led his cowboys into town either. Each was strong on his own ground.

The third element, and a very recent development, was that goddamned John Slocum, a hired gun if Gould ever saw one. Hogan had brought him in, that much was clear. He'd been clever about him, bringing him in as a wagon driver. He'd managed to slip him past Gould that way. He'd even allowed Slocum to get robbed once, really throwing Gould off guard. That was a dirty damn trick, Gould thought.

Then he'd pretended to fire Slocum in front of a whole crowd of citizens. At that point, Slocum had really seemed to be a loner with no stake at all in what happened in Joshville. The only hint that he might turn out to be a problem had been his friendship with that Running R cowboy, and Gould had not taken that too seriously.

He'd sent those stupid assholes to suggest to Slocum that he not get himself involved in local politics, but that had backfired. Slocum was tough. Gould had to give him that. But what was really worrying him was that all of his enemies seemed all at once to have joined forces. And Slocum was right there in the middle of it all. Slocum was the magnet drawing them all together.

He had not, after all, broken with Hogan. That had all been a sham. Slocum and Hogan were still in cahoots. And then Slocum and that damned cowboy had high-tailed it out to the Running R in the company of those two damned whores. That meant that Reed was an ally. Slocum and Hogan and Reed, all together, all lined up against him. The situation was getting out of hand, and something drastic would have to be done soon.

Gould jumped when he heard the knock on the outside of his office door. He shouted too quickly.

"Who is it?"

He knew that his voice and the quickness of his response betrayed his fear, and he knew too that he had to regain his composure. He couldn't afford to let anyone see his fear and anxiety. He had to be in control. Everyone out there had to know that he was in complete control, just like always before. He took a deep breath and exhaled slowly.

"It's Red," came the answer.

"Come on in."

The door opened slightly, and Red poked his face in timidly.

"Smitty said you wanted to see me."

"That's right," said Gould, his voice betraying impatience. "I said come in, didn't I? Come on in. Come on. And shut the door behind you."

Red did as he was told, and stepped up close to the big desk.

"I'll get right to the point," said Gould. "We got to do something, and we got to do it fast."

"We only got three men, Boss," said Red. "Four if you count Brady."

"Brady don't count for shit," said Gould. "But if we

don't stop Slocum and Hogan and Reed right now, we're going to lose this town.''

"We could take Hogan out real easy," said Red. "Right now if you want."

"No, you damn fool," Gould snapped. "That would be too obvious, and it would for sure set off Reed and Slocum. We ain't strong enough to stand up to them just now. We got to have some more men."

"I could hire on some guns over to Wagon Gap, I think," said Red. "If not, I know I could get some over to Rocky Meadows. How many you want?"

Gould's face twisted as he mulled over the answer to that question. He thought about the pile of money in his safe, and the thought of paying a large sum out in gunfighter wages pained him. Still, something had to be done. It would take an army to attack the Running R, and it would take a good deal of his fortune to pay an army. He wondered how long it would take to build it back up again after he had won the fight.

Maybe fewer men could handle the job, though, if they went about it in the right way, just going after Slocum and Reed. With those two gone, Hogan would fall easy. And Slocum and Reed could both be taken out of town, with no hostile witnesses.

"Six men," said Gould. "Six good men. No goddamn slouches, you hear me? Six damn good men."

"Reed's got twenty cowhands out at his ranch," said Red. "We can't take them on with only six more men."

"We ain't going to try, you dummy," said Gould. "We ain't going after no twenty cowhands. They ain't nothing without a boss, are they?"

"Well, no," said Red, scratching his head. "I reckon not, but—"

"All we're going after is just two men," said Gould.

"Just two men. Slocum and Reed. With no bosses left around to pay their wages, them twenty cowhands will leave the county to look for work. Just only two men is all we got to get. Do you think that nine of you could maybe handle that little job?"

"It'll take me a couple of days to hire six men," said Red. "Another day to get back with them."

"Well, get started then," said Gould. "But before you leave town, send Brady and Smitty and Orren over here to me. You hear?"

"Yeah," said Red. "I'll get on it right now."

Red left the office, and Gould settled back in his chair with a heavy sigh. He thought about Hogan and Reed and Slocum, and he thought about Slocum and that damned cowboy leaving town with those two whores.

"Shit," he said out loud. "Goddamned whores."

They were good-looking women, though. He had to admit that. He wondered what Slocum and the cowboy were doing with them out there on the Running R, and as his imagination roamed, his right hand drifted down below the roll of fat hanging over his belt. Slowly he began to rub at the bulge in his trousers, and he felt his cock rise.

He stroked it up and down until it pushed hard at his trousers crying out for some room in which to grow. He opened up his fly and let it out. He couldn't see it there below his belly fat, but he could feel it. He thought about the two whores, and he gripped his cock between his thumb and two fingers, and he began to jerk it up and down.

He had not ever had either one of the two whores, for the last time he had been with a woman, he had not been able to get so much as a rise out of his treacherous prick. He had been too embarrassed to ever try it again. He pictured the whores, imagining them undressed, and he hated them, and he wanted them, and he imagined himself on top of first one of them, then the other, banging away at their sloppy cunts. He jerked himself faster and faster, and his breathing was hard and fast.

And then he tried to picture the two women, their hands tied behind their backs. They were on their knees, their faces on the floor, and he was behind them, flailing away at their round butts with a wide leather belt.

He pictured the red welts across their white asses, and he imagined their cries and pleas, and he jerked his prick faster and faster, and then he shot his wad, the first spurt landing on some papers on top of his desk, the second, slower and weaker, hitting his trouser leg. After that, the remainder dripped down onto the seat of his chair between his legs.

There was a knock on the door, and he realized that it was unlocked.

"Just a minute," he shouted, and he tucked his already limp prick back into his trousers, feeling the final dribbles on his leg and in his pants. He fastened his fly and took a deep breath, trying to compose himself.

"Come in," he said.

It was Brady who opened the door and stepped in first, followed by Smitty and then Orren. Gould realized that, with Red out of town, as he should be already, or would be very soon, this was his entire force, and a sorry force it was.

"Red said you wanted us," said Brady.

"That's right," said Gould. "I sent Red out of town. Till he gets back, you're it. The three of you. I want all of you to stick with me like glue till I say otherwise. You got that?"

"You expecting trouble?" Brady asked.

"Slocum's up to something with Reed and his bunch," said Gould. "Of course I'm expecting trouble. They ain't out there having no dance party." He shifted his broad ass in the big office chair. It was sticky inside his pants. "Smitty," he said, "go get me a bottle and a glass and bring them in here."

Smitty left the office, and Brady stepped up close to the desk, his face showing fear.

"Mr. Gould," he said, "you don't think they'll come in here shooting, do you?"

"I don't know what to think," said Gould. "I can't read their damn minds, now can I? All I know is they're after me. They've joined forces. That's all I know, except that you're all the protection I got. So we stick together. Close. Understand?"

"Yeah," said Brady, "but—

"But what?"

"Well, why'd you send Red off then?"

"I sent Red off, you dumb, log-headed son of a bitch, to hire some more men. That's what I sent Red off for. And till he gets back with them, I want you three right here with me. Any more stupid questions?"

"Well, but shouldn't I be over at the jailhouse?" Brady stammered. "I am the marshal, and it might not look right, me not being in my office. You know?"

"You're the marshal 'cause I made you marshal," said Gould, "and I made you marshal 'cause you work for me. And as long as you work for me, you'll do what I say. Now sit down over there and shut up."

Brady sat, and Smitty came back in with a tray. It had a bottle and four glasses on it, and he carried it to Gould's desk and set it down. Gould grabbed the bottle and poured himself a drink. Smitty reached for the bottle then, but Gould slapped his hand.

"Ow," said Smitty.

"You all need to stay clearheaded," said Gould. "No drinking."

As Smitty sulked his way to a chair, Gould tossed down his drink. It choked him, and he was seized by a violent fit of coughing.

12

Merv was lurking in the dry arroyo, still unable to decide what to do about his situation. He had no idea what had become of the gunfighter. The man could be waiting for him on the road or back in town. He was afraid to ride out in either direction. He was tired and hungry and thirsty. He had seen a jackrabbit, but he had been afraid to shoot at it for fear the gunfighter would hear the shot and come after him. He wanted to get back into town some way and find Gould and demand some help. A hideout or some money to travel on or the protection of the rest of Gould's gang. He was going to have to do something soon. Anything would be better than hiding in this damned arroyo. Well, almost anything.

He heard the sound of approaching hoofbeats, and he started to turn his horse and flee deeper into the wash. But he changed his mind. It might not be the gunfighter. It might be some of his pals. Or it might be some passing traveler he could rob. He checked the six-gun at his side and found it ready. Then he dismounted and sneaked to the edge of the wash to watch.

Red was not riding hard, for he had a long ride ahead of him, and he wanted to save his horse. It was a hostile country for a man afoot, and he sure didn't want to put himself in that kind of trouble. He thought about his mission, and he considered riding on west, not stopping in Wagon Gap or Rocky Meadows or any damn place until he was well away from Joshville and Gould and all the trouble with Slocum and Hogan and Reed and his ranch hands. Gould was scared. Red had seen that in him, and if Gould was scared, there had to be good reason for it.

Gould's money was pretty good, and Red hated to leave that behind, but it sure as hell was not worth dying for. Then again, if he did as Gould had told him to do, they would be strong again, and maybe everything would be back the way it had been before.

Well, he decided, he would ride on into Wagon Gap and have a look around. See who might be available over there. If he didn't find who he needed, he would check at Rocky Meadows. If he located and managed to hire enough men, he would go back to Gould. If not, he would just ride on and let Gould worry about Slocum and all the rest. If it came to a choice between Gould's desires and the safety of his own hide, well, then, Gould be damned.

Merv peered over the edge of the arroyo like a frightened mouse. He saw the rider coming, closer and closer. He was afraid that he would be seen, and so he thought about dropping down out of sight until the rider passed him by, and then he recognized Red. He scampered up the side and out of the wash, shouting in his glee.

"Red. Hey, Red. It's me. Merv. Goddamn, am I glad to see you."

The suddenness of Merv's appearance and his shouts frightened Red's horse. It reared and snorted, and Red was almost unseated. He fought the animal as Merv rushed toward them, still waving and shouting. At last both men managed to calm the beast.

"Damn, Merv," said Red. "You damn near got me throwed, boy. What the hell you trying to do?"

"Sorry, Red," said Merv. "I didn't mean to, but I got excited. I'm just so glad to see you. I been hiding out here ever since we got ambushed. I ain't et a bite since yesterday noon. Man, I'm starving and thirsting both at the same time."

Red pulled loose his canteen and tossed it to Merv, and Merv gulped greedily before handing it back. "You got anything to eat?" he asked.

"Yeah," said Red, "but this ain't a good place to stop. You got a horse?"

"He's down in the wash," said Merv.

"Go get him," said Red. "We'll ride up to the creek ahead and stop a spell."

They found a place beside a narrow, winding creek where they could sit behind some boulders and be out of sight of anyone who might be traveling the road, and they dismounted there, letting the horses drink. Red pulled some hardtack and jerky out of his saddlebags and gave them to Merv. Merv ate like a wild animal.

"We heard what happened out here at Bald Knob," said Red. "You been in that arroyo ever since then?"

Merv continued eating, but grunted an affirmative answer to Red's question. Red was thinking about how Gould had ordered the killing of Sam, the last known witness to the robberies. Gould had hinted that he wanted Red to ride out and locate Merv and kill him too, if he wasn't already dead. But he'd never actually issued the order. He'd changed his mind quickly, and his next actual order had been the one sending Red to Wagon Gap and maybe on to Rocky Meadows.

Red wondered if he ought to go ahead and shoot Merv and get it over with. He didn't really want to. Gould had sent him out to raise some men, and here was Merv. On the other hand, Merv was known by Slocum to be one of the bandits. He was the last possible link between Gould and the holdups. Well, Red would think on it for a while.

Merv wiped his mouth with a sleeve. "Damn, that's better," he said. "I didn't know what the hell to do. I didn't know whether that bastard was looking for me or waiting along the road or what."

"You mean Slocum?" asked Red.

"Yeah. That's his name. I couldn't think of it, but it was him all right."

"Was anyone with him?"

"I never seen anyone but just him," said Merv. "Slocum."

"I wouldn't have thought just one man could have done it," said Red. "Just only Slocum, all by hisself."

He thought about the six men he was supposed to hire for Gould, nine men altogether to fight Slocum and probably Reed and all his cowhands. It had sounded reasonable, the way Gould had put it, but sitting out here alone with Merv and thinking about Slocum all by his lonesome wiping out the gang of road agents, he wasn't so sure.

"How'd he manage it, Merv?"

"Hell, I don't know," said Merv, shaking his head.

"He just come out of nowhere and started shooting, and he shot everyone except me. I was around on the other side of the curve out of sight, you know, where we wait for the wagon? I just lit out as fast as I could go."

Red sat silent in deep thought for a space. The situation was out of hand, and he didn't know what to do. He knew what Gould would have said. Kill Merv and ride on over to Wagon Gap to hire six men. Six men. Hell, Slocum alone had taken five men.

"Say," said Merv, interrupting Red's reverie, "where you headed out this way all by yourself?"

Red looked at Merv. He and Merv were alike. They could understand one another. Gould, on the other hand, was something else. Red felt no affinity for Gould, only for his money.

"Merv," he said, "whenever you all got most nearly wiped out by Slocum, and whenever you didn't show up, Gould just damn near sent me out to find you and kill you."

Merv stared at Red, unbelieving. "Kill me?" he said. "What for?"

"Sam was the only one brought in alive," Red continued. "They had him in a jail cell, and Gould had him killed so he couldn't talk. You're the only one left."

"Well, I wouldn't talk," said Merv. "Why would I?"

"I guess Gould just didn't want to take no chances."

"Well, that fat son of a bitch," said Merv, his anger rising suddenly. "That double-dealing fat bastard. Wait a minute. You ain't thinking —"

"I ain't going to kill you, Merv," said Red. "If I was, I wouldn't have told you."

"What are you going to do?"

"I was headed for Wagon Gap," said Red. "Maybe on over to Rocky Meadows. Gould sent me out to hire six new gunfighters. I told him that Reed's got twenty cowhands, but he said we could get by with six, said all we're going to do is just kill Slocum and Reed. The others will all be easy once them two's gone. That's what he said.''

"That damned Slocum can take on six just by his-self,''

said Merv.

"Yeah," said Red. "I'm thinking about just riding on. You ever been to Californee?''

"No. I ain't.''

"You want to ride out that way with me?''

"It's an idea," said Merv.

"It don't seem like a bad one just now either," said Red. "The only thing is—I just hate to ride away from all that money ole Gould's got stashed in his safe.''

"Yeah," Merv mused. Then he suddenly perked up. "Say," he said. "I got an idea.''

"What is it?''

"Suppose we was to go on over to Wagon Gap, like you said, maybe on over to Rocky Meadows. Only thing, we don't just hire on six men like Gould wants. We hire on twelve—or twenty.''

"Gould said only six," said Red.

"What can he say if we ride into Joshville with twenty men? You reckon he'd stand there in front of twenty gunmen and tell fourteen of them to get the hell out of town? The fat son of a bitch wanted you to kill me. Right? Let's kill him, and let's us take over using his money.''

Red rubbed his chin and his eyes opened wide. It was an alternative he hadn't considered, and it didn't seem like a bad one at that. He thought that between Wagon Gap and Rocky Meadows they ought to be able to come up with twenty men. He wondered, though, how much money there would be by the time they split it up that many ways.

"Twenty more cuts out of ole Gould's money will sure shorten the shares," he said.

"Hell," said Merv, "some of them won't live through the fight."

"That's right," said Red. He stood up and dusted off the seat of his britches. "Let's do her, by God."

Merv grinned wide and stood facing Red. He reached his right hand out, and they shook on it. "Damn right," he said. "Let's do 'er."

It was late afternoon, and Slocum had spent much of the day scouting the area around the line shack. He had seen no sign of any of Gould's bunch anywhere near the Running R, and he had taken note of the comforting fact that, except for the rising Titty Hill to their rear, the view from the shack was long and clear. Anyone approaching from most any direction could be seen long before he would arrive at the shack, and an approach from the rear over the top of Titty Hill was unlikely.

He returned to the shack, took care of his horse, and went inside. Francine and Jessie had seen him approach, watching through the window, and as he stepped inside, Jessie put a cup down on the table.

"Fresh coffee," she said, "or would you rather have something stronger?"

"Coffee sounds real good right now," said Slocum. "Thanks."

He hung his hat on a peg on the wall, and removed his gunbelt and carried it with him to the table. He slung the gunbelt over the corner of the back of a chair, then sat down.

"You see anything out there?" Francine asked.

"Nothing that didn't belong," Slocum said, and he picked up the cup and sipped hot coffee. "That's good."

"Glad you like it," said Jessie, "and I'm glad you're back."

"Me too," said Francine. "It's lonesome way out here. And boring. And it's a little . . ."

Slocum waited for her to finish, but she seemed to have stopped. "A little what?" he asked.

"A little scary, I guess," she said.

"Tell you what," said Slocum. "In a little while, we'll go outside and take a look at the side of the hill back there behind us. I'll bet we can find a good hiding place out there. And if you'll take a look out the window, you'll see that no one can come up on you by surprise. You can see forever. So if you should see someone coming, and you don't like his looks, you'll have plenty of time to get out and hide. Take a look."

Francine walked over to look out the window. She leaned on the sill and stared out, sweeping the horizon with her eyes. Slocum was right. She did feel as if she could see forever. She swept the skyline from left to right and then back again. This time she saw something. Just a speck. She watched it for a moment to be sure, and then she knew that it was moving.

"John," she said. "Someone's coming."

Slocum got up from his chair and moved to the window to stand beside Francine. Jessie had come up right behind him.

"What is it?" she asked.

"It's a rider, all right," said Slocum. "Coming this way."

He walked over to the other side of the door, where his Winchester leaned against the wall, and picked it up and moved back to the window. The rider was closer but still a silhouette.

"Who is it?" asked Francine.

"Can't tell yet," said Slocum, and he rested the barrel of the Winchester across the windowsill. The rider came closer. They waited. Then Francine shouted out with delight in her voice, "Hey. It's Curly Joe." Slocum squinted and waited as the rider moved even closer, but Francine had hurried over to the door and jerked it open, waiting to greet the cowboy. At last Slocum was able to make him out. She had been right.

"By God, gal," he said, "you got good eyes."

"That ain't the only thing good I got," said Francine.

"You sure are right there," said Slocum, "and I'll fight anyone who says different." He lowered his rifle and leaned it against the wall, then went back to the table to lift his cup and sip from it again. Soon Curly Joe rode into the yard and dismounted. Francine ran out to meet him, throwing her arms around his neck and giving him a warm, wet kiss full on his lips. Jessie followed her outside, and a moment later Slocum stepped out the door.

"How'd you get away in the middle of the day?" he asked.

"The boss sent me out," said Curly Joe. "He wants all of you to come to dinner at the big house tonight."

"All of us?" asked Jessie.

"That's what he said. He told me to ride up here and bring you all on down to supper. That's what he said."

"You have any idea what for?" Slocum asked.

"If I was to have to take a guess," said Curly Joe, "I'd say he wants to talk about this Gould business. I heard him send a couple of the boys into town to fetch out Hogan too. That'd be my guess. Well, I'll hitch up the wagon for you ladies to ride in, and then we can be on our way.''

''Right now?'' said Francine.

''It'll be supper time by the time we get there,'' said Curly Joe.

''Come on, Francine,'' said Jessie. ''We can be dressed by the time he's got the wagon hitched.''

Slocum was already throwing the saddle onto the back of his big Palouse when he heard Curly Joe walking up behind him.

''They looked dressed to me,'' said the cowboy.

Slocum gave a shrug and reached down to tighten the cinch. ''You can't never tell about women,'' he said.

13

Jessie and Francine had picked out their plainest dresses, but they still were conspicuous at the big table in the ranch house, for their plainest was none too plain. But everyone was polite to them, including Reed and his wife Myrtle. Slocum had wondered if there was a Mrs. Reed. Now he knew. Her hair was gray, but she was certainly a handsome woman for her age. Ranch life had not worn her down. Not so you'd notice.

The meal finished, Reed ordered coffee poured all around. Slocum thought that it was about time for something a bit stronger than coffee, but he didn't say anything. He sipped at the coffee.

"I guess you're all wondering why I asked you here tonight," Reed said. Everyone looked at the tough, old rancher. Slocum noticed that the man had a strong, rugged look about him, but he noticed something else, something in the eyes, the expression on the man's face. He was an honest, hardworking man, a man who had built his own empire without trampling on the rights of others. Slocum would have bet a month's wages on that.

"I reckon," he said, "that it has something to do with the mayor of Joshville."

"You're right about that, Mr. Slocum," said Reed. "Of course, our opposition to Gould is the only thing that all of us here have in common. Our reasons may be different, but we all have some reason to want the man out of office and out of power."

"I'd say clean out of the state," said Francine.

"Mr. Reed," said Hogan, "I think that Gould is already out of power. I don't believe he has more than four men around him anymore, and one of them's Brady. Any power that he has left is nothing but the power of intimidation, and I damn sure won't be intimidated."

"Well, Mr. Hogan," said Reed, "that's good to know, but I didn't call everyone here to plan an assassination. That's Gould's way, not mine, and I hope it isn't the way of anyone here at my table. I chose to run for the office of mayor of Joshville as my way of attacking Gould, and without any solid evidence of criminal activity on his part, that's still the only strategy I can justify."

"Then why are we here?" said Slocum. "I ain't carrying no campaign posters."

"I didn't expect you to," said Reed. "Your dealings with Gould have been different from mine. I know there have been some fights. I'd like to hear about them from you, and I'd like to know whether or not either of you have any evidence against Gould that would hold up in a court of law."

"I've got nothing but strong suspicion," said Hogan. "Oh, hell, I know he's guilty as sin, but if you want to talk legalities, then, no, I ain't got nothing on him."

"Since you put it like that," said Slocum, "I guess I

ain't either. Noting but what you might call—circum-stantial.''

"Just what kind of circumstantial evidence do you have, Mr. Slocum?" Reed asked.

"Oh, mostly just who his associates are, I guess. We seen that fellow Waters with Gould, and then Waters was with the road agents who held up Mr. Hogan's wagons.''

"And Gould's been trying to buy me out," said Hogan.

"That's suspicious," said Reed, "but not necessarily incriminating. Anything else?"

"Well," said Slocum, "when Gould seen me drinking with Curly Joe there, he suggested that I leave town. Then his bodyguards jumped me and tried to convince me.''

"And while that was all going on," Curly Joe added, "Brady stood by watching. We know that Brady's Gould's man.''

"That's it?" said Reed, obvious disappointment in his voice. No one spoke. "Well, we need some solid evidence that will hold up in court. In the meantime, all we can do is hope that I can win this election.''

"How much time until the voting?" Slocum asked.

"Fourteen days from today," said Reed.

Slocum shook his head. "Seems to me," he said, "you need to get to stumping.''

"You're right about that," Reed agreed. "First thing in the morning, I'm calling the boys together and asking for volunteers. I won't send any man out to campaign for me unless he wants to do it, but any who are willing, I'll send out in groups of four to ride out and talk to the voters.''

"Hell, Boss," said Curly Joe, "every one of the boys will ride out for you. I guarantee it."

"That's good to hear, Curly Joe," said Reed. "Still, I'll ask them in the morning."

Slocum finished off the coffee in his cup, and was thinking that he'd heard enough of this bullshit about courts and politics. He'd handled the road agents his way, which was what Hogan had hired him to do, and he was just about ready to take care of Gould the same way.

"More coffee, Mr. Slocum?" Mrs. Reed asked.

"Well, uh . . ."

"Perhaps Mr. Slocum would like something a bit stronger, Myrtle," said Reed. "I have a very good brandy, Mr. Slocum."

"Thanks," said Slocum. "A good bourbon would be just the thing."

"I can handle that too," said Reed, but as he was about to push his chair back, Mrs. Reed stood quickly.

"I'll get it, dear," she said, and went to a nearby cabinet to pour the drink.

"Say," said Hogan, "I saw something today that everyone here ought to know about."

"Go ahead, Mr. Hogan," said Reed.

"Gould's man Red rode out of town this morning headed toward Wagon Gap."

"Alone?" Reed asked.

"All by himself."

"I wonder what that means," Reed mused.

"Might be he quit and headed out," said Curly Joe. "From what you said a while ago, the odds ain't in their favor no more."

Mrs. Reed put a glass of whiskey on the table in front of Slocum.

"Thank you, ma'am," he said.

"Could be," said Hogan. "I told you Gould's down to a slim crew. Maybe ole Red pulled out, like you say."

"Or maybe he went to hire more men," said Slocum, "to shift the odds back in their favor again." The table grew quiet at that somber thought, and Slocum sipped his drink. It was a good bourbon, one of the best he'd ever had. That was just what he would have expected from Reed.

"Mr. Slocum's right, of course," said Reed. "That's a distinct possibility. And I believe that we need to know for sure what Red is up to. Curly Joe, send out a couple of boys in the morning to trail him and see what they can find out."

"I'll do 'er, Boss," said the cowboy.

That last proposal was a little more to Slocum's liking. At least it was doing something. He'd have ridden out of this damn country several days ago and forgotten all about all of them except for two things. One was his firm conviction that Gould was indeed behind the freight wagon robberies, and therefore he didn't feel that he'd yet fulfilled his obligation to Hogan. The second was the fun he was having with Jessie—and Francine.

For Slocum was a man of action, and if there was a job to be done, he wanted to be doing it, not sitting around jawing about it. Either that or get the hell out and forget about it. He tipped up his glass and emptied it.

"Mr. Reed," he said, "if it's all right with you, I'd like to ride along with those boys."

"You're welcome," said Reed. "And thanks."

Jessie looked at Slocum with a disappointed expression on her face, and Francine seemed almost in a panic. Their looks did not go unnoticed by Slocum.

"You suppose, Mr. Reed," he said, "that Curly Joe could stay with the ladies until I get back? I don't like to think about leaving them out there all alone."

Reed's face flushed, and he stammered. "Well, I, uh, I suppose so," he said. "I suppose that would be appropriate under the circumstances."

Curly Joe did his best to keep a serious face, as if his mind would be only on business. No one was fooled, though.

14

Early the following morning, Slocum rode away from the Running R in the company of two young cowboys called Billy and Slim. Curly Joe was at the line shack with the two women, and Slocum had a pretty damned good idea what they were up to in his absence. He recalled the fun he'd had alone with the gals and smiled.

"Mr. Slocum," said the cowboy called Slim, "Red's got a hell of a start on us, ain't he? Shouldn't we be riding along a bit harder?"

"Let's take it easy," said Slocum. "He'll get to Wagon Gap before we do no matter how hard we ride, but we'll get there, and we'll figure out what he's up to. We won't kill our horses in the process either."

"He's right, Slim," said Billy. "Ain't no use in hurrying."

"I reckon so," said Slim.

Slocum took stock of the two cowboys. They were both young. Likely they weren't even old enough to vote for their boss in the upcoming election. Slim's nickname suited him. He was tall and lanky. The gunbelt he wore around his skinny waist looked to Slocum like it would fall down around his ankles if the boy got off his horse and stood up straight.

Billy, on the other hand, was maybe a head shorter than Slim and carried a good, solid-looking body. He looked like he'd be a good scrapper. He also wore a gunbelt, and Slocum wondered whether or not either kid could handle the six-shooter he toted. They were both nice, polite young men. They probably wouldn't have been able to keep their jobs with Reed if they'd been otherwise.

They sure did talk a lot, though. Slocum figured that must have something to do with their age, and he tried to recall if he had been that way himself. He didn't think so, but then, his own youth had been severely interrupted by the damned Civil War, or the War Between the States, depending on who you were talking to. Well, he'd try to dismiss their jabbering as due to their age and upbringing. Then Billy started to sing a song, and Slocum surprised himself by thinking that it was a pleasant diversion.

"Get out the way of Old Joe Clark," Billy sang. "Hide that jug of wine. Get out the way of Old Joe Clark. He's no friend of mine."

They passed one of Hogan's wagons along the way, but other than that, the day was uneventful. They stopped and made a camp for the night a few miles short of Wagon Gap. The next morning, they rode into town early.

Wagon Gap was a busy little town, and Slocum had wondered why since the first time he had seen it. There were a few little businesses, but for the life of him, he couldn't figure out where all the people came from. He'd seen other towns like that, though, towns that made him wonder why they ever got established and just what the hell kept them going.

"Where to, Mr. Slocum?" Billy asked.

"Let's find us some breakfast," said Slocum.

Riding slowly down the main street in search of a place to eat, Slocum noticed a number of tough-looking rannies hanging around. If Red had come to Wagon Gap in search of toughs and gunnies, he would probably have no trouble picking up all he thought he needed.

They hitched their horses to a rail outside a place called Jodie's Eats and went inside. Greasy smoke filled the air in the small room. The place was crowded, but they managed to find an empty table. Surprisingly soon, a hefty, middle-aged woman wearing a grease-stained apron approached them to take their orders. She brought coffee back right away, then disappeared into the hazy atmosphere.

Slocum looked over the crowd, and his impression was much the same as it had been out in the street. Wagon Gap was full of men who thought they were tough and would probably have been bought easy for a job of pushing their weight around. He had, as yet, seen no sign of Red. In a few more minutes, they had eaten their greasy meals, paid for them, and gotten back out onto the street.

"By God," said Slim, "I swear that I will never again complain about Cookie's meals. If ever I do, Billy, kick my ass and then remind me about this breakfast we just had."

"I can't kick that high," said Billy, "but I'll for sure remind you. Better yet, I'll just tell Cookie what you said, soon as we get back to the ranch."

"No," said Slim. "I wish you wouldn't tell Cookie."

"Well, I'm going to."

"Boys," said Slocum, "I think I'll cross the street and stroll down to the far end. If you all will do the same thing on this side, I'll cross back and meet you down there."

"We looking for Red?" Billy asked in a near whisper.

"Or anything else of interest," said Slocum, and without another word he started across. He had to dodge a rider moving too fast, and then he had to wait for a wagon to roll past. Across the street, he stepped up onto the board sidewalk. He waited for two men walking shoulder-to-shoulder to get on out of the way. Then he started moving toward the far end of the street.

He had gotten about halfway when the sound of his name startled him. He turned to find himself facing a bearded man wearing a black hat and vest. He wore two low-slung Colts around his slim waist, and he grinned at Slocum through his whiskers. There was something familiar about the man, but Slocum couldn't quite pin it down.

"Do I know you?" Slocum asked.

"Abilene," said the man. "About ten years ago, I'd say."

Then it all came back to Slocum. The beard was new since then. That was what had thrown him off. The man was a gunslinger with a reputation for taking any job that paid and for always finishing his job. He had tried to get Slocum to work with him back then, and Slocum had refused. He found the man's line of work and his attitude toward it unsavory.

"Jasper Cummings," Slocum said.

"That's right," said Cummings. "Goddamn. What a surprise to run into you here like this. Come on, Slocum. Let me buy you a drink."

"It's a little early in the morning, Jasper," said Slocum.

"Well, hell," said Cummings. "A cup of coffee then."

Slocum didn't like Cummings, and any other time would almost certainly have turned him down. But something told him to play along. He glanced toward the far end of the street, and saw Slim and Billy just arriving and looking around. He didn't want them to walk in on his scene with Cummings, and wondered what he might do to prevent that from happening.

"Where to?" he said.

"There's a place right across the street," Cummings said, and he gestured toward Josie's.

"I just had breakfast there," said Slocum, "and I still stink of grease."

Cummings shrugged. "Well," he said, "there's Big Ed's down at the far end of the street. It's a bar, but they serve coffee too. It don't stink of grease."

Slocum could see Slim and Billy walking back. "I'll meet you down there in a couple of minutes," he said. "I want to bring my horse down."

"You ain't trying to skip out on me again, are you?" Cummings asked. "Like in Abilene?"

"I didn't skip out on you, Jasper," said Slocum. "I just told you that I wasn't interested. I'll be down at Big Ed's directly."

Cummings stood silent for a moment, then shrugged again. "Yeah," he said. "All right. I'll see you there."

Slocum waited until Cummings had started walking toward Big Ed's, and then he walked back across the street to the rail where he and the two cowboys had tied their horses. He fiddled with the cinch until Billy and

Slim walked up. He didn't look up from his pretend work, and he spoke in a low voice.

"Boys," he said, "make out like you don't even know me. I'll get back to you some way."

He took the reins of his big stallion loose from the rail, swung up into the saddle, and rode toward Big Ed's. The two cowboys did not watch him. They tried to do as he had told them to do, pretend to be totally disinterested. Billy leaned back on the rail.

"What the hell do you reckon that was all about?" he said.

"I don't know," said Slim, "but I'd say he's onto something."

"I reckon you're right," said Billy. "Well, what do you want to do now?"

"We don't know what Slocum's up to," said Slim, "but we know what the boss sent us to do. Let's wander around and see if we can spot ole Red."

Cummings poured some whiskey into his coffee and held the bottle over the table toward Slocum.

"No, thanks," said Slocum. "The coffee's fine like it is."

Cummings shrugged and put the bottle on the table. Then he lifted his cup for a long sip.

"It's better like this," he said, "but suit yourself. Listen, Slocum. Ever since the first time I run across you, I've wanted to work with you. You and me would make a hell of an unbeatable team."

"No one's unbeatable," said Slocum.

"Well, by God," said Cummings, "you and me would come as close as any. Closer. I mean it." Slocum sipped his coffee and kept silent. "You turned me down flat in Abilene," Cummings continued, "but I ain't holding no grudges for that. I still want to team up with you, and I'm going to give you another chance. What do you think about that?''

''What's the deal?'' Slocum asked.

Big Ed's was not busy. There was really no one within earshot of normal conversational voices. Still, Cummings leaned confidentially forward and lowered his voice.

''There's a fellow in town hiring guns,'' he said. ''He works for an ole boy over in Joshville. The mayor. It seems the mayor is about to lose his hold on the town, and he wants to firm up his grip. Get it?''

''You can stop right there,'' said Slocum. ''I know just who you're talking about, and he won't hire me.''

''How come?''

''I was working for his opponents,'' said Slocum. ''Not as a gunhand. I was driving a freight wagon. When I found out I was smack in the middle of a feud, I pulled out. That's what I'm doing here in Wagon Gap. I'm on my way out of this country.''

''Well, hell, boy,'' said Cummings. ''You wasn't a part of the fight. Ain't no reason for them not hire you on.''

''They'd associate me with the other side,'' said Slocum. ''They wouldn't trust me.''

''Let me talk to the man who's hiring,'' said Cummings.

''Who is he?''

''Calls himself Red. If I heard another name I can't recall it.''

''I know him,'' said Slocum. ''I had a fistfight with him. He was trying to run me out of town for his boss.''

''A fistfight ain't nothing,'' said Cummings. ''Let me talk to him.''

"I don't know, Jasper," said Slocum. He shook his head. He hadn't planned it this way, but a scheme was shaping in his head. "His boss sure ain't got no use for me. I better just ride on out of here."

Cummings suddenly grew even more conspiratorial, leaning in closer to Slocum and lowering his voice even more. "Listen to this," he said. "The boss—what's his name?"

"Gould," said Slocum.

"Yeah. That's the son of a bitch," said Cummings. "Gould. Gould's money is hiring us, but what he don't know is that he's going to get cut out of the whole damn deal. So it don't make a shit what he thinks about you."

"What do you mean he's getting cut out?" Slocum asked. This was starting to sound interesting.

"Red and another fellow came in here to hire me on," said Cummings. "Fellow called Merv. Anyhow, Red explained the whole deal, and then he said that him and Merv are planning to get rid of Gould and take over. They said that he wouldn't be no problem at all."

"I see," said Slocum.

"But that ain't all I got to tell you, pardner," said Cummings. "The way I see it, Red and Merv ain't no problem at all for the likes of us. They get rid of Gould, and then we get rid of them, and then the whole damn setup belongs to you and me. Didn't you ever want to own a whole goddamned town?"

"I never thought of it before," said Slocum.

"Well, think of it now. Why should a fat-assed son of a bitch own a town just because he has the money? Especially when he needs men like us to hold onto it? If we're the ones who can get it and hold it, then by God let's take it all."

"It's an interesting proposition, Jasper," said Slocum,

"but as far as I'm concerned, it hinges on you being able to convince Red to take me in on the deal."

"Leave that to me," said Cummings. "I'll convince the son of a bitch."

"I'll meet you back here this evening," said Slocum. "You can tell me how it all turned out."

After wandering the streets of Wagon Gap aimlessly, not really knowing what they were looking for, and wondering just what the hell Slocum was up to, Billy and Slim rode back to the campsite where they had spent the night before. It was early evening, too early to hit the sack, but they had grown weary of the busy little town.

"What the hell are we going to do, Billy?" Slim asked.

"I don't know," said Billy. "Ole Slocum told us to act like we don't know him, so we can't very well ask him what he's up to. I don't rightly want to ride back to the ranch and tell the boss that we just come over here and left Slocum and that's all."

"Me neither," said Slim. "And if you ain't got no better idea, I'm going to lay out my roll and get some sleep."

"It don't seem right," said Billy, "but I ain't got no other idea. Go on ahead. I guess I'll build a little fire and make some coffee."

The sun had gone down. Billy was sitting by the fire sipping from a tin camp cup, and Slim was snoring in his bedroll. Billy heard the sound of approaching hoofbeats. He put his cup down and eased the six-gun out of his holster, ready for whatever might come. He was facing the town and the approaching horse. He waited. Then he recognized the big Palouse and then the rider.

"Slocum," he said. "Come on in. You want a cup of coffee?"

"I'll take one," said Slocum, swinging down out of the saddle. "Thanks."

Slim rolled over mumbling, raised his head and saw Slocum there, then sat up rubbing his eyes. "Howdy, Slocum," he said.

"Howdy, boy," said Slocum. "It's a good thing for you I'm friendly."

"Hell," said Slim, "Billy was watching."

Billy poured a cup for Slocum and then another for Slim. "Well," he said, "what's up?"

Slocum took a sip of the hot coffee and wondered why it always tasted better outside. "I want you two to get a good night's sleep," he said, "and then get an early start back to the ranch."

"You ain't riding with us?" Slim asked.

"Nope," said Slocum. "I've got a new job." He told them about his chance meeting with Cummings and the offer Cummings had made him. He told them about Red's plan to double-cross Gould and Cummings's plan to double-cross Red and Merv.

"It's getting to where a fellow can't trust no one," said Slim.

"Well," said Slocum, "I'm trusting you two to get back to Reed just as fast as you can and tell him what's going on here. Tell him to get ready for anything. They're raising a small army here, and I'm going to be riding with them. I'll try to let someone know what the plans are, but I might not be able to get away just any time. So you all have got to be armed and ready. You got all that?"

"Yeah," said Billy.

"I got it," said Slim. "It's going to be a fight, ain't it?"

"It's going to be a fight for sure," said Slocum, "and it's likely to be a big one. Have someone tell Hogan too. He might want to get out to the ranch for a spell just for safety."

"We'll tell him," said Billy.

Slocum finished off the coffee in his cup, put the cup down, and stood up to walk back to his waiting horse. He swung up into the saddle.

"See you down the road," he said.

"Good luck to you," said Billy.

"To all of us," Slocum said.

15

Slocum walked into Big Ed's and found Jasper Cummings sitting at a table with Red and Merv. The latter two scowled as they saw Slocum approaching the table.

"Is that the man you were talking about?" Red asked Cummings.

"That's him," said Cummings. "There ain't a better man with a gun around—unless it's me."

"Forget it," said Red. "I know him. I don't like him, and I don't trust him."

"I know him too," said Cummings, "and I want him in. Hell, boy, with me and Slocum along, you don't need anyone else. Just the two of us can handle any job that comes along."

"I said forget it," snapped Red. "I'm in charge of this show, and I ain't hiring Slocum." He looked up at Slocum, who had by this time reached the table. "Just run on along, Slocum," he continued. "Cummings here made a mistake."

"Sit down, Slocum," said Cummings.

Slocum pulled out a chair and sat, and Cummings shoved a glass and a bottle toward him. Slocum poured himself a drink. Red watched the whole business, seething inside. He knew how tough Slocum could be, and he had a pretty good idea about Cummings. Still, he knew that he had to maintain control of the situation. He glanced over at Merv, who had sat silent throughout the whole episode. He could see that Merv was nervous. Well, hell, so was he. His palms were sweating.

"Cummings," he said, "you got to remember who's the boss here. Who's doing the hiring. Only one man can give the orders here, and that's me. I say Slocum ain't going to be hired on, and if you can't live with that, well, then I reckon you ain't hired either."

Cummings smiled, and Slocum sipped his whiskey. Merv sat stiff and scared.

"There's something you don't understand, Red," said Cummings. "Me and Slocum, we decided it earlier today. You ain't calling the shots no more. We know what the game is, and we know where it's being played. We don't need you."

Sweat ran down Red's face. "You're making a mistake, Cummings," he said. "Gould sent me to hire men. You ride in there without me, and he won't have nothing to do with you. You need me to get to Gould's money."

"I don't think so," said Cummings. "What do you think, Slocum?"

"I don't think Gould gives a damn whose gun he's buying," said Slocum. "Red. You. Me." He shrugged and lifted his glass for another sip. "Even this road agent here."

"And especially," said Cummings, "if I ride in there and tell him how you was planning to take over from him."

"You agreed with me on that," said Red.

"Well, I ain't going to tell him that part," said Cummings. "Not right away."

Red considered his options. He was in a bad spot, and he knew it. He could just get up and walk away, maybe hire some more gunnies. The problem with that was that he was damn near sure that he couldn't find any to match Cummings and Slocum. He could get up and walk away and forget the whole thing. Ride on out of the damn country. It wouldn't be the first time he'd let himself get run out of town. But he was broke, or damn near so, and back at Joshville a whole possible empire waited. He wanted at least a piece of it.

He considered challenging Cummings, and then he thought about being dead. Merv likely wouldn't raise a hand to help. That option seemed to be not really an option at all. Only one course remained open to him. He would have to swallow his pride.

"All right," he said. "You want to run the damn show, it's yours. Hell, I ain't never been in charge of nothing before in my whole life. I probably wouldn't be no good at it anyhow."

"Then you agree that Slocum's in?" Cummings asked.

Red shrugged. "Whatever you say."

"All right," said Cummings. He reached for the bottle and began pouring drinks all around. "Let's celebrate. But not too long. We'll be heading for Joshville early in the morning."

They had a couple of rounds before Cummings excused himself to go out back to relieve his bladder. "Keep an eye on our new partners here," he said to Slocum with a smile.

Slocum waited until Cummings had disappeared. Then he casually reached for the bottle.

"How many other men have you recruited?" he asked Red.

"None," said Red. "Cummings told me he'd round up all we needed."

"Who has he got?"

"Just you," said Red. "That's all I know. We'll sure need some more, though, especially if Reed and his bunch decide to get in on it."

"Don't say anything to Cummings about Reed," said Slocum.

"Why not?"

"First of all," said Slocum, "I think that we can handle anything that comes up. There's four of us, and Brady and those other two back in Joshville with Gould. In the second place, if we add more men, we wind up dividing the shares that many more ways."

"Yeah," said Red, "but Reed's got twenty cowboys out there on his ranch."

"They're cowboys," said Slocum. "They ain't gunfighters. Besides, who was it all by himself took out that whole damn gang of road agents you had robbing the freight wagons?"

"He's right, Red," said Merv. "He got them all but me, and I run like hell."

"All right," said Red. "I won't say nothing." It was tenuous, for sure, but it felt good to have an ally against Cummings, even on such a small matter. It made Red feel a bit more secure. "Say, Slocum," he said, "all them things I said about you before, forget it, huh?"

Slocum sipped his whiskey. "It's all forgot," he said.

• • •

When the others had gone to bed, Slocum rode again out to the camp to see Billy and Slim. He found both cowboys waiting with guns drawn.

"It's just me, boys," he said, "but I'm glad to see you alert. I want you to head on out tonight. If you go slow and easy you shouldn't have any problems. The road's a pretty good one."

"What's up?" Billy asked.

"The gang's headed for Joshville in the morning," said Slocum. "I want you two to be well ahead of it. By the way, it looks like there's only four of us after all."

"That's some comfort," said Slim.

"One's Jasper Cummings," said Slocum, "and he bears watching."

"And one's you," said Billy, "so there's really only three."

"And four more back in Joshville," said Slocum.

"Them four ain't much," said Slim.

"Don't seem like it," said Slocum, "but never underestimate your enemy. If he's too weak to fight you, he might slip up and hit you in the back of the head."

"So what do we do, Slocum?" Billy asked. "If there's only three of them here, we could lay an ambush in the road somewhere along the way."

"You could," said Slocum, "and it ain't a bad idea, but I don't think your boss would go for it."

"He's right," said Slim. "Mr. Reed wants everything to go by the law."

"Just ride on back to the ranch and tell Reed what all we found out and what I'm up to," said Slocum. "That's all."

He waited and watched as the cowboys saddled their broncs and tied their bedrolls behind the saddles, then mounted up and rode toward Joshville. They'd be back at the ranch by morning, by the time Slocum and the others started toward Joshville, and Reed and Hogan and the rest would know what was going on. The odds weren't too bad if and when it came to a fight, but Slocum knew that was not the problem.

Reed would not be satisfied without proof of wrong-doing on the part of Gould and his gang. That would be up to Slocum. In his role as a gang member, he would have to find the proof. That done, Reed could decide on the good and proper course of action. Slocum would just as soon have taken the advice of the cowboys and set up an ambush to get the whole damn thing over with. But hell, he told himself, this ain't my show. He turned his horse and headed back toward Wagon Gap.

With Slocum well on his way and the cowboys even further along on their way, a lone rider moved out from behind the darkness of a clump of trees. Jasper Cummings smiled after Slocum. He's up to something, he told himself. I wish I knew what the hell it was. He urged his horse forward and moved onto the road.

Ignoring Slocum for the time being, he headed toward Joshville, following the two cowboys. He rode easy for a time. The road twisted and curved, and he was in no hurry. Then he topped a rise, and down below, the road was long and straight, and he could see them ahead clearly in the bright moonlight.

He halted his horse, turned it sideways in the road, and dismounted. He pulled a rifle out of a saddle boot and laid it across the saddle. Taking careful aim, he sighted in on the back of one of the riders. He squeezed the trigger and the boom of the big rifle resounded through the night air.

•   •   •

Billy jerked once with the impact of the bullet, died instantly, and fell forward on the neck of his horse. Slim heard the boom of the rifle and saw Billy slump. Even so, it took a moment for the reality of the situation to sink into his mind. He reached over to help Billy, calling his name, and he realized that Billy was dead. Something tore at his left shoulder, and then he heard the boom again. He yelled, and kicked his horse into a run.

He hated running off from Billy like that, but there was nothing he could do for him. Billy was dead. Billy was dead, and someone was trying to kill him too. There was another shot. He had no idea how close that one might have come. He was racing ahead in the darkness, racing for his life. He could feel the warm blood running down his arm, and he lashed at the little cow pony underneath him.

"Shit," said Cummings. He shoved the rifle back into the boot and swung himself up into the saddle. Jerking his horse around, he raced after the remaining cowboy. Down in the valley, the road was darkened by tall trees which grew on either side and obscured the moonlight. He lost sight of his prey. At last he slowed, then stopped.

It wasn't worth ruining his horse, and it wasn't worth the time it would take to catch up to the man. He needed to get back to town, to the hotel. He needed to get to his room and get some sleep. He had said that they would leave early in the morning, and he wanted to be the first one up and ready.

It would have been better if he had killed them both, but after all, he didn't really know what Slocum had told them or why. He just knew that Slocum was up to something, was trying to put something over on him, and he had no intention of letting that happen.

He was a little disappointed. He had really almost allowed himself to believe that he and Slocum would actually be working together at last. He admired Slocum as he had admired few men in his lifetime, but he well knew that Slocum had never liked him.

He had thought for a while that he had found a deal so sweet that Slocum could not resist teaming up with him. It had seemed so. He had even imagined that once they had taken over Joshville, they would really be partners, and Slocum would get to like it, would get to like him. And he realized that a part of him still held out hope for that possibility.

But he knew that Slocum was dangerous, and he knew that he would have to watch him carefully. Cummings had no idea why Slocum had sneaked out of town to meet the two cowboys or what Slocum had told them. He only knew that he didn't like it. It didn't bode well for their future partnership.

Perhaps it had been harmless after all and everything would work out for the best. Even so, he wished that he had killed them both. He wondered. If Slocum was trying to warn someone, who would he be warning? Gould? It didn't seem likely that Slocum was allied in any way with Red and Merv. Then it would have to be the enemies of Gould, the ones that Red had been sent to recruit guns to fight against.

He tried to recall just what Red had told him about the situation in Joshville. Gould was the mayor, and a rancher named Reed was challenging him. Could Slocum be working for Reed? It was possible. Thinking back, Cummings realized that it had been all too easy for him to talk Slocum into joining up with him on this deal. He decided that he would have a private talk with Red when he got back to town.

16

Curly Joe couldn't believe his good fortune. He had actually been ordered by his boss to spend the night with the two women at the line shack. Of course, he knew that Reed would never have agreed to the arrangement if Slocum had not practically insisted on it and if Reed had not felt the need of Slocum's help in the fight against Gould. Still, it was damn good luck, and Curly Joe was determined to take advantage of it.

And the ladies too were thrilled. Even in peaceful times they'd have been frightened at the prospect of staying the night alone in the shack far from civilization. And Curly Joe was a nice young man and, Francine thought, a hell of a good romp. It made the time pass more quickly and much more enjoyably.

The first night, Jessie had turned in early, feigning near exhaustion. That had left Francine and Curly Joe to their pleasure, and Jessie had lain awake for what had seemed like hours listening to the two of them get it on. Had they really believed that she was asleep? How could anyone have slept with all that going on? Still, she had pretended, and the next morning no one had said anything about it at all. They had had their breakfast about the middle of the morning, and around noon a cowboy had come riding up with some supplies for the cabin sent over by Reed.

"Any word for me?" Curly Joe had asked.

"Just stay here and keep an eye on the ladies," the cowboy had said. Then, making sure the ladies were not near enough to hear, he had added with a wink, "You want to change jobs with me today?"

"Naw," Curly Joe had said. "Much as I'd like to be riding herd with you, Mr. Reed said I should stay here, and that's just what I aim to do."

"You want I should ask him to send me back up here to give you a hand? 'Pears to me like you could use some help."

"Get on out of here," Curly Joe had said, and the cowboy had ridden away laughing.

They spent the rest of the day talking about what Slocum might be doing and what might happen when he returned. They talked about Reed's chances in the coming election, and they worried, especially the ladies, about the possible violence in the near future.

That evening, Francine decided to go to bed early, but she wasn't interested in sleeping. She pulled Curly Joe toward the bed, tugging at his shirttail and trying to get the shirt off over his head. Curly Joe resisted. Looking over his shoulder at Jessie, he protested. "Francine."

"Don't mind me, sugar," said Jessie. "You two lovebirds just go right on ahead and take your pleasure."

That was all the encouragement Curly Joe needed, and he and Francine were both naked in a minute. She lay back on the bed and spread her legs, revealing her dark bush for his eager eyes. His eyes weren't all that was eager, though. She watched as his cock slowly grew and stood at attention right there before her. She held out her open arms.

"Come on, baby," she said. "Come to Mama."

Curly Joe moved between her legs, and she reached for his rod with both her hands. She grabbed it and stroked it, and then she ran its head up and down the wet and silky walls of her cunt. He held himself aloft, letting her take charge. Then she guided his cock into just the right place and thrust upward with her hips. He drove down deep into her warm, wet cavern.

Their bodies slapped against one another in happy unison for a moment, and then Francine wrapped her arms around Curly Joe and rolled him over until she was on top. She kissed him eagerly, lolling her tongue around the inside of his mouth, and then drew her knees up under her so that she could sit up, still impaled by his hard and throbbing cock.

Upright, she rocked her hips forward, sliding on his wet skin. "Ah," she moaned, and she rocked back and forward again, faster and faster, and then with a loud moan of relief, she relaxed and fell forward heavily on him. She raised her head and looked into his face smiling.

"Damn, that was good," she said.

"Already?" Curly Joe asked in amazement.

"Hell, yes," she said, "and ready to go again. I can go like this all night long. Or at least, as long as you can last."

She rocked again and came again, and Curly Joe thought that maybe he could last all night in this position. He was damn sure going to give it all he had. He reached up with both hands, taking a sweaty tit in each, and gave them a gentle squeeze. Francine shivered with her whole body, and Curly Joe tried to thrust upward into her, but with her whole weight sitting on him, he was already about as far inside as he could get.

Then Francine looked over at Jessie, sitting alone on the far side of the room, and she had an idea.

"Jessie," she said. "Come on."

"You're doing all right," said Jessie.

"I'm screwing him," said Francine, "but I ain't doing much with his face. Why don't you come and sit on it?"

Jessie thought about Slocum. If she joined in on this, she would feel as if she had betrayed him. Then she realized that she had not felt guilty about getting into bed with any man since . . . Well, since a hell of a long time ago. She laughed at herself, tossed her head back, and stood up.

"Sure," she said. "Why not?"

She pulled her clothes off quickly, flinging them aside, and soon Curly Joe saw her dark love triangle looming very near his face. Jessie leaned over, taking his face in her hands, and kissed him full on the lips. It was a long kiss and a deep one, and while it lingered, Francine rocked furiously back and forth on his upright rod.

Then Jessie broke the kiss and straightened up. She put one knee on the bed beside his head, then the other, and then she spread her legs and lowered her crotch until the hairs tickled his face. She lowered herself further, and Curly Joe felt the wet kiss of her cunt all over his face, and his tongue shot out in response.

Down below he felt Francine stiffen again, and he heard her moan in pleasure. Then she relaxed, as before, but when she fell forward, she was embraced by Jessie.

They were both still for a moment, holding each other tightly. Then they looked each other in the eyes, and then they kissed, gently, tenderly at first, then more passionately as their lips parted and their tongues fought their way past each other to feel around inside each other's mouth.

Together, as if on cue, they began to move their hips slowly, rocking back and forth, Jessie rubbing against Curly Joe's face, feeling his tongue flickering against her, Francine once again riding the stiff rod. And then they came together, and then they broke the kiss.

"Trade places?" offered Francine.

"Sure," said Jessie.

The switch was quickly accomplished, and as soon as Francine lowered her crotch onto his face, Curly Joe reached around to take a cheek of her ass in each of his hands. She rubbed hard against him, and he wondered for a moment if he would be able to breathe.

Just then he felt his cock being sucked in, deeply embraced by Jessie's cunt, and he felt Jessie's weight settle down against his hips and crotch. He thrust upward with all his might, and as he did, Jessie began rocking back and forth. Curly Joe worked hard, trying to satisfy both cunts at the same time, and then the women came together again, embraced again, and kissed again.

"Let's let him up," said Jessie, and she swung her leg over his face as if she were dismounting a horse.

"Okay," said Francine, sliding slowly backward off the still-swollen cock. When it at last slipped loose to flop against his belly, she leaned forward and took it in her hand.

"Where do you want to put it, honey?" she said.

Curly Joe gasped for breath.

"I want to fuck you like a dog," he said. "Both of you."

Jessie and Francine looked at each other, smiled, then dropped to their hands and knees side by side. Curly Joe looked at the two marvelous asses staring him in the face. Quickly he moved in on Francine, driving into her cunt from the rear. When he had shoved his full length into her, she giggled and wriggled her ass. Curly Joe gripped her by the waist and began to drive into her as hard and fast as he could.

Suddenly on the backstroke, he pulled all the way out and moved to Jessie. She arched her back in response to his thrust, and he pounded into her again and again.

Francine rolled over onto her back and moved her head up against Jessie's thigh to gain a wondrous view of what was happening. She was looking up from almost underneath Jessie's belly, looking between Jessie's legs to where Curly Joe's cock was driving in and out.

"Oooh," she said.

She watched the heavy balls swing back and forth in their sack as Curly Joe banged away at Jessie's backside. Suddenly Curly Joe stopped thrusting. He stiffened all over.

"Oh," he moaned. "Oh."

Jessie turned her head to look back at him.

"You coming, honey?" she asked.

"No," he said. "No. Not yet, but I'm fixing to."

Francine scurried out from under Jessie's belly, getting back up on her hands and knees, but facing the other direction, her head pressed against Jessie's ass.

"Put it right in here, honey," she said, and she opened her mouth wide.

Curly Joe pulled out of Jessie's cunt, and Jessie fell over on her side. Quickly Curly Joe moved in on Francine, and she eagerly sucked in his cock, wet with the juices of her own and Jessie's cunts. She sucked deep and squeezed hard with her lips as she withdrew. Curly Joe shuddered. He knew that he would shoot his wad at any moment. Francine sucked his entire length into her mouth again, and as she did, Jessie crawled around behind Curly Joe. She got up on her knees just in back of him.

Francine pulled away again until only the head of the swollen cock was between her puckered lips. As she started forward again, taking it in again, Jessie reached with both hands to grab Curly Joe's balls from behind. The shock of it caused Curly Joe to thrust forward, ramming his full length into Francine's mouth. Francine squeezed with her lips, trying to hold the rod in place. Jessie clutched the balls and scratched with her nails, and Curly Joe thrust again and again and again, and then he felt the pressure deep inside turn loose, and he sent gush after gush of rich, thick cum juice down the waiting throat of Francine.

She waited for him to be still and for the throbbing of the cock to stop. Then she slipped it out of her mouth and milked it like a cow's tit, licking the last drop off the head. With a gasp of near exhaustion, Curly Joe fell over onto his back. Covered with sweat, he lay there with his mouth wide open sucking air.

Francine lay down beside him, allowing her legs to flop apart. Still upright on her knees, Jessie looked down into the eyes of Francine, and Francine smiled. Then Jessie leaned forward until her hands were on the bed, and she crawled up between the open legs and lowered her face slowly until she pressed into the warm, wet muff of Francine, and Francine moaned happily and squeezed the cheeks of her ass together and thrust up-

ward with her crotch into Jessie's face. And using the
fingers of both her hands, Jessie dug into the soft, wet
lips and spread them, and then she reached with the tip
of her long tongue to just the right spot, a spot she knew
well, and Francine writhed and moaned and whimpered,
and in spite of himself, Curly Joe sat up wide-eyed to
watch as Jessie drove deeper with her fingers and lapped
more quickly with her tongue. And then Francine stiffened and twitched and screamed or moaned or screamed
and moaned at the same time, and it was so loud that it
frightened Curly Joe. He thought that it might have been
heard way back at the ranch house. And he watched as
Francine relaxed and closed her eyes and smiled con-
tently, and down below Jessie only nuzzled gently at the
muff.

"Goddamn," he said.

Jessie turned her head to look at him.

"I never seen anything like that before," he said.

Jessie noticed that his cock was about half risen.

"Did it get you excited, cowboy?" she asked, reaching for the cock and gripping it hard. It throbbed in her
hand and stiffened and grew some more.

"Yeah," said Curly Joe. "It did."

She used the cock like a handle, pulling herself toward
him, rising up onto her knees. He got up onto his own
knees facing her, waiting for her to come closer. She
moved in close, and her lips brushed his, but they did
not kiss as she passed him by, moving around behind
him and pulling him close to her, his back pressed
against her breasts, his ass pressed against her still-damp
crotch. Her arms circled him and held him tight, and
then one hand gripped his cock and began to stroke it
back and forth. With the other hand she tickled his balls.
He started to protest that he wanted to screw, but the

hand was jerking him off faster and faster, and he was liking it, and he kept quiet and let it go until he sent forth a great shot that splattered just between the tits of Francine, and another that landed on her belly. The next went into the hairs of her crotch, and the last several dribbled along her inner thigh.

Moving around in front of him, Jessie squeezed the last drops into her own palms, then leaned over the still-relaxed Francine and began rubbing all of the drops into Francine's lovely, white, smooth skin.

17

Slocum took his horse back to the livery stable in Wagon Gap, put him in a stall, fed him some oats, and rubbed him down real good. He took his time. The horse deserved special care and attention. At last Slocum was ready to go back to his hotel room and get at least a few hours sleep in a bed, but just as he was about to head for the front door of the stable, he heard a horse approaching. He ducked back into the stall with his big Palouse and waited.

In another moment, Jasper Cummings came riding into the stable. Slocum waited until Cummings had unsaddled his mount before stepping out of the stall into the open hallway.

"You're out late, Jasper," he said.

Cummings turned quickly to face Slocum. Then he relaxed and smiled. "You too," he said. "Where'd you go?"

"I went out for a short ride," said Slocum. "What'd you do? Follow me?"

"Follow you?" Cummings laughed. "Hell, no. I just went out for a short ride myself. That's all."

Slocum didn't believe Cummings for a minute, and he wondered if the gunfighter had followed him to the camp. If so, had he gotten close enough to hear what was said? If Cummings had managed to hear what Slocum had said to Slim and Billy, then he was onto Slocum's game. And if he had followed him but not heard the conversation, then why was he not questioning Slocum about his meeting with the cowboys? Slocum couldn't figure out what was going on, but he knew that something was wrong. He and Cummings were obviously playing a cat-and-mouse game with each other. He wondered how long it would go on.

Deliberately turning his back on Slocum, Cummings finished tending to his horse. Then he turned around slowly and deliberately. "Since we're both up," he said, "let's go have a drink. I'm buying."

"It's late," said Slocum, "and you said you wanted to get an early start in the morning."

"Hell, I can drink all night and still start out with the sun. I can go for a week without sleep and ride from here to California. What's the matter, Slocum? You getting old? Slowing down?"

Slocum stared at Cummings. Just what was the man up to anyway? What were the words he was not quite saying?

"I reckon I can keep up with you," he said.

"Let's go then," said Cummings.

They walked down the dark street to Big Ed's, and found it still open and still lively. It was no longer crowded, though, a significant number of its patrons having staggered home or passed out. They got a bottle and two glasses, found a table, and sat down. Cummings poured the drinks and pushed one toward Slocum. He picked up his own glass and lifted it as for a toast.

"Here's to our partnership," he said, and he smiled a broad, genuine-looking smile. Slocum thought, if I didn't know the son of a bitch, I'd believe him. He lifted his own glass halfheartedly, playing the game. "You know, pardner," Cummings continued, "I've been looking forward to this for a long time. Ever since Abilene at least."

"Yeah," said Slocum, "you said that before."

"I'm a patient man," said Cummings. "Hell, I waited, and look what's happened now, all these years later. I finally got what I wanted." Slocum sipped his whiskey, watching Cummings closely, expecting anything. "You know," Cummings went on, "my old daddy, he was a hardworking son of a bitch, he was. He was a college professor, he was. Did I ever tell you that before?"

"No," said Slocum, "you never."

"Well, he was. Professor of Greek and Latin. The classics, they call it. Back in Ohio. I was sure as hell a disappointment to him. I was too wild and rowdy. He was forever getting me out of one jam or another. Trying to get me to settle down and study hard and make something of myself. Finally, I was about fifteen, I guess, I told him one day, I said, 'Daddy,' I said, 'I'm heading west, and there ain't a damn thing you can do to stop me.'

"Hell, I braced myself then. I didn't know what he might try. I thought he might try to whip my young ass, big as I was. I hadn't yet got my full growth yet, though, and I didn't know but what he could still do it. Then I thought he might go for the law or something like that. Try to get me locked up. But he didn't do neither one

of them things. No, sir. You know what he done, Slocum? The one thing I never anticipated. You know what
he done?''

"I got no idea, Jasper," said Slocum.

"Son of a bitch cried," said Cummings. "He cried.
He didn't break down and bawl. Nothing like that. But
tears rolled down his cheeks. Both sides. I seen them. I
sure never expected that.'' Cummings tossed down his
drink and poured himself another. "Then he said to me,
'Son,' he said, 'be careful. You might just get your way
one of these days.' ''

"What do you reckon he meant by that?'' Slocum
asked.

Cummings shoved the bottle toward Slocum, and Slocum poured himself another shot.

"I wondered about it off and on for years after that,''
said Cummings. "It was a long time before it made any
sense to me. But I think what he meant was that a man
can think he knows what he wants until he gets it. Then
he finds out what all is really involved in it. Get it? You
understand?''

"I ain't sure," said Slocum. "I didn't grow up with
no professor.''

"Well, think of it like this," said Cummings. "Suppose you're looking off in the distance at a big-ass
mountain, and you're thinking that more than anything
in the world you'd like to be up on top of that mountain.
So you head for it, and it's a hell of a lot farther off
than it looked like it would be. Before you get there,
your horse drops dead underneath you, but you keep
going.

"Finally you reach the foot of the mountain, and you
look up, and goddamn, you can't even see to the top,
but you start climbing anyhow. You've forgot just about

everything else. All you want is to be on top of that mountain. You climb and climb. Your fingers is bleeding. Your knees is skinned up. The soles of your boots is wore out and your feet's blistered. You keep climbing.

"Farther up, the air's thin and it's hard to breath. There's snow on the ground and it's cold. But you keep climbing, 'cause getting to the top of that mountain has become the whole purpose of your life. You following me?"

"Yeah," said Slocum. "I think so."

"Then you get there. You actually make it to the top. It's the thing you've wanted more than anything else. You get there, and then you see seventeen of the biggest, meanest goddamn grizzly bears you've ever seen in your life, and they're coming right at you."

Slocum nodded his head and murmured a noise of understanding as he lifted his glass to sip.

"Or say you see this woman," said Cummings. "She's young and beautiful and well mannered and rich. Everything you could ever want in a woman. You decide you have to have her. You go courting, but she won't have anything to do with you. And why should she? She's so far above you in every way that you ought to be ashamed of yourself for even thinking about her. But you keep after her anyhow. You won't quit. And finally, in spite of all logic, she accepts you, and you get married and move into a nice little house with her, and she turns out to be the most godawful nagging bitch on the face of the earth."

"I got the point, Jasper," said Slocum.

"Did you?"

"Yeah. I got it."

"You real sure, Slocum?"

"I don't need no more stories."

"Back in Abilene," said Cummings, "I wanted you to be my pardner. You turned me down. I kept on wanting that, and by God, yesterday I made you a proposition, and you accepted me. I got what I wanted."

"Just what the hell are you getting at, Jasper?" said Slocum.

"Oh, I guess I got to watch out for them grizzlies," said Cummings. "That's all."

"Is that what you were doing tonight?" Slocum asked.

"You might say that."

"You followed me. Didn't you?"

"Yep."

"And what did you see?"

"I seen you meet with them two cowboys outside of town."

"And?"

Cummings shrugged.

"Did you sneak up and listen to what we had to say?"

"Didn't get that close," said Cummings. "Just seen you meet with them. That's all."

"Listen here, Jasper," said Slocum. "I said I'd work this job with you. I never said I'd answer to you for every move I make. If you don't trust me, then let's just forget the whole damn thing. I didn't come to you asking for this deal. Remember?"

"Who were those boys, Slocum?" Cummings asked.

"Just a couple of cowboys I know," said Slocum. "It don't matter none. It's got nothing to do with our deal."

"They ride for the Running R?"

"What's the difference?"

"The difference is that one of them got away."

"What?"

"I think you heard me."

"You killed one of them?" Slocum asked.

"I meant to get them both," said Cummings. "I was too far back. When I dropped the first one, the other one took off like hell. So whatever it was that you told them, one of them's still alive to tell it to someone else. Who's he going to tell, Slocum?"

"You shot him from behind?" Slocum asked. "You backshot him?"

"It don't matter to a dead man which side he got shot from," said Cummings. "What matters right now is which side you're on, pardner."

Slocum realized that he had seriously underestimated Jasper Cummings. He had thought that Cummings was so tickled to have him as a partner that he wouldn't be watching him closely. He had thought that Cummings would trust him. That mistake had cost one of the young cowboys his life. Slocum's mistake. He wondered which of the two cowboys Cummings had killed. Which one his own mistake had killed.

He also wondered if there was any way to save this situation, and he decided that, with Cummings, there was not. He could try to make up some reason for his meeting with the two cowboys, but Cummings wouldn't believe anything he might say at this point. It was also possible that Cummings really had overheard the conversation and was still playing his game with Slocum, waiting to catch him in an outright lie.

On top of all that, Slocum was suddenly sick of playing the game. Even if he could manage to come up with some tale that Cummings would accept about why he had met with the two Running R cowboys, he knew that he would not be able to stomach riding along with the backshooting bastard long enough to finish the game.

He felt his lips twitch and curl involuntarily, and he stared hard into Cummings's face.

"The game's over, you dog puke," he said.

Cummings smiled, and the smile looked so warm and genuine that Slocum thought he would have believed anything the man might have said to him had he not known him so well. Then Cummings placed both hands on top of the table in plain sight and slowly and carefully pushed back his chair. He stood up and moved away from table and chair, giving himself plenty of room.

"No," he said. "It ain't over yet. Not quite."

"Then it's your move," said Slocum.

As quietly as this confrontation had developed, it had not escaped the notice of the other patrons of Big Ed's, and all eyes in the place were on Cummings and Slocum. Slocum wanted badly to kill Cummings, but he didn't want any trouble at Wagon Gap over the killing. He would not make the first move.

"Get up," said Cummings.

"I said it's your move," said Slocum.

"I don't want to kill you sitting down."

"It didn't bother you to shoot a man in the back," Slocum said.

"You're different, Slocum. Get up. We'll make it a fair fight."

"Go to hell, where you belong."

Slocum wondered if he was playing a fool's game. Cummings was good. He knew that. And all things being equal, a man standing certainly had the advantage over a man sitting down. But he knew that he was needling Cummings, and he was enjoying it. He also knew that he could get his Colt out pretty quickly, even from his seated position. He saw Cummings's right hand twitch, and he knew that the man was getting nervous.

"Get up, Slocum," said Cummings. He was no longer smiling.

"Jasper," said Slocum. "You ain't worth standing up for."

Cummings's hand went like a blur for his revolver, and Slocum flung himself to his left, landing hard on the floor and pulling his Colt as he fell. Cummings's shot roared in the big room of the saloon, and the lead smashed into the wall behind where Slocum had been sitting. Slocum fired from the floor, one shot. The bullet smashed Cummings's sternum.

Cummings stood still for an instant, a surprised expression on his face. He looked down at the dark splotch on his shirtfront. His hand relaxed, and he dropped his gun with a clatter. He stood weaving for a moment, and his legs became rubbery. Then he dropped to his knees, then fell forward to land hard on his face, and then he moved no more.

18

The line shack was closer than the ranch house, so Slim
decided to stop off there. He knew that he should go
directly to the ranch house to report to Tobias Reed, but
he had ridden hard almost the distance from Wagon Gap.
He was afraid that his horse would drop out from under
him if he pushed it much further, and he was not doing
so well himself.

He had lost blood from the wound to his left arm, and
he was tired from the long hard ride. He figured that he
had better stop at the line shack or he might not make
it at all.

Curly Joe was sound asleep, naked in bed between two
beautiful naked women, and his dreams were wonderful
ones, even more wonderful than the reality of the night
before. Something shook him halfway out of his happy
dreamland, and he fought it, but it shook him harder,
and then a voice intruded into his magic world.

"Curly Joe," said Jessie. "Wake up, damn it. Someone's outside."

Curly Joe sat up quickly with a perplexed expression on his face. "What?" he said.

"Someone's outside," Jessie repeated.

Francine popped up then, her eyes wide with fright. "Oh, God," she said. "Do something."

Curly Joe suddenly came wide awake and jumped out of the bed. He ran across the room to where a rifle leaned against the wall. Jerking it up, he cranked a shell into the chamber and stepped over to the door, opening it just a crack. He looked out, and saw Slim sagging in the saddle, blood soaking his left arm.

"It's Slim," he said. "He's hurt."

Curly Joe put the rifle aside and ran out the door. Still naked, he helped Slim down out of the saddle.

"Come on, pard," he said. "We'll take care of you."

"Billy," said Slim. "They shot Billy off his horse. Billy's killed."

"Who shot him?" asked Curly Joe.

"I don't know," said Slim.

They had reached the door by then, and Curly Joe helped Slim on inside.

"We'll talk about it later," he said. "Let's get you fixed up first. Come on, pardner. Come on."

The two cowboys were moving toward the bed. Jessie and Francine, holding the sheet up to cover their nakedness, looked at each other.

"They're coming over here," said Francine.

"Say, Curly," said Slim, "you're nekkid."

"I was asleep," said Curly Joe.

"Oh," said Slim. "You sleep nekkid?"

"Shut up," said Curly Joe. "Look out, girls."

He was about to dump Slim onto the bed, and Francine and Jessie both squealed and jumped out of bed at once. As weak as he was, Slim could not help but react.

"Goddamn," he said. "You're all nekkid."

Curly Joe dropped Slim onto the bed, and Slim groaned as he hit. Curly Joe began tearing at the wounded cowboy's shirt sleeve. "Give me a hand, girls," he said.

"Well, give us a chance to get dressed," said Francine.

"He can't wait," said Curly Joe. "Pull off his boots, and boil up a pan of water."

Soon Slim found himself being tended to by three naked nurses, and even in his dazed condition, he found it very amusing. He wished that he had strength enough to laugh, but he also knew that he had something very important to tell, and he was afraid that he would drop off to sleep.

"Listen to me," he said. "I got to tell you what happened."

"It'll keep," said Curly Joe. "You need to rest."

Jessie and Francine were getting their clothes on, but Curly Joe was still naked. He was sitting on a chair beside the bed.

"No," said Slim, "it won't keep. Shut up and listen to me. Slocum found an ole boy in Wagon Gap who's rounding up a small army for Gould. He joined up with them to kind of spy on them. He said they'd be heading for Joshville this morning. He told us to get on back and let the boss know what was happening so's we could be ready here for whatever might come. Well, he went back to Wagon Gap, and we headed back here, but along the way, someone ambushed us. Shot Billy in the back. Nicked me, but I got away. Come straight here. You need to get on into the ranch house and tell the boss.''

"Yeah," said Curly Joe.

"I'd get some clothes on first, though, if I was you."

"Oh, hell," said Curly Joe, reaching for his jeans.

"Wait a minute," said Francine. "You ain't going to leave us here with just him. Not with an army coming, you ain't."

"You'll be all right," said Curly Joe, pulling on his boots. "They'll be headed for Joshville."

"Can you be so damn sure of that?" Jessie asked.

Curly Joe hesitated and looked at Slim. Slim just shrugged, as much as he was able.

"I'll get the wagon hitched up," Curly Joe said. "We'll all go together to the ranch house."

Slocum was up early, but even so, when he headed for Big Ed's he found Red and Merv waiting for him in the street. They didn't look quite ready for a fight with Slocum, but they did look pretty damn sullen.

"You killed Cummings," said Red.

"You heard about that already," said Slocum.

"Hell," said Merv, "it's all over town."

"I ain't had no coffee," said Slocum. "Let's go inside and talk it over."

Red and Merv looked at each other. They had both been on the wrong end of a fight with Slocum. Red shrugged, and they followed Slocum into Big Ed's, where they found a table and ordered up a round of coffee. As soon as the coffee was delivered, they ordered breakfasts.

"What's this all about, Slocum?" Red asked.

"He pushed me," said Slocum. "Besides, you know how he was already trying to take over from you. I didn't like the way he done that."

"What do you care what he was doing me?" Red asked.

"Ain't no love lost between us," Merv added.

"That's got nothing to do with it," said Slocum. "We all agreed. We had a job to do, and we was all in it together. We hadn't even got started, and he was already trying to take over. I figured if you couldn't trust him, neither could I. You got to know you can trust your partners, like them or not."

"That makes sense, Red," said Merv.

"Another thing," said Slocum. "There was two Running R cowboys in town yesterday."

"What was they doing here?" said Red. "Spying on us?"

Slocum shrugged. "I don't know," he said. "They might have been. But that ain't the point. The point is that Cummings went out and shot one of them in the back last night. That was a stupid move on his part. If Reed thinks that we've started shooting his boys, that will give him an excuse to start shooting back. So I killed Cummings, and on our way back home today, we'll pick up the cowboy's body and deliver it to Joshville. We'll have Brady ride out to the Running R and tell Reed what happened. His boy got shot in Wagon Gap, and the man that done the shooting is dead. That'll be the end of it."

Red wrinkled his face in deep thought for a moment. "Okay, so what do we do now?" he asked. "There's only just three of us now."

"There's four more back in Joshville, ain't there?" Slocum said. "That makes seven."

"Smitty, Orren, Brady, and Gould," said Red. Merv was counting on his fingers.

"That's seven, all right," said Merv.

"Brady ain't much," said Red, "and Gould always hires someone else to do his fighting for him. That only leaves five that's worth a damn in a fight."

"Listen," said Slocum. "There won't likely even be a fight. Tobias Reed and his cowboys are the only ones that we have to worry about, and Reed wants everything done by the law. That's why Brady's important. Brady's the marshal. Reed ain't going to send his boys against the law. All we got to do is watch things until the election's over, and as long as Gould wins, everything's okay. Ain't no sense in taking a goddamned army into Joshville. It costs too much money."

Merv leaned over close to Red's ear and spoke in a low voice. "He's right, Red. Besides, he's like a damned army just all by hisself. I seen him in action."

Red sipped his coffee and pondered the situation for a moment. "So," he said, "just the three of us is going back to Joshville?"

"Well, I ain't the boss here," said Slocum, "but that would be my notion."

"All right," said Red. "Hell, I came out of there by myself. I'm going back with two more."

"There's another thing," said Slocum. "I know you was planning to take over from Gould." Red stiffened, but Slocum pretended not to notice. "We take an army back there, there's no telling how many of them would follow you and how many would back Gould up. After all, he's the bank."

"That's right," said Merv.

"It's a whole lot safer this way," said Slocum.

Tobias Reed stepped out on his porch when he heard the wagon coming. It was coming fast, and his first inclination was to fire the hand who was driving the wagon. He recognized the two women first, and then he saw that Curly Joe was driving. He stepped down off the porch to meet the wagon, as Curly Joe stopped it in a cloud of dust. He opened his mouth to shout, but Curly Joe shouted first.

"Boss," he yelled, "there's a whole army of gun-slingers coming from Wagon Gap. They done killed Billy, and they shot Slim here."

Reed noticed then for the first time that Slim was laid out in the bed of the wagon. He didn't hesitate. He shouted orders to everyone in earshot.

"Get Slim into the house. Get every man armed. Watch all the roads into the ranch. Set out sentries. Get to moving. Get to moving. And take care of them horses."

Every hand on the ranch was running. Soon every cowboy was at least wearing one six-gun and carrying one rifle. The Running R was ready for a major assault.

When things were finally prepared to the satisfaction of Tobias Reed, and the atmosphere had settled down to a quiet but tense calm, Reed called Curly Joe over to his side.

"The ladies will stay in a guest room in the house," he said. "We'll keep Slim in the house too till he gets better. You'll move back into the bunkhouse. You did the right thing, Curly Joe, bringing them all in here."

"Thank you, Boss," said Curly Joe. He didn't really like the prospect of moving back into the bunkhouse after the time he had enjoyed in the line shack, but the times did seem to demand a change.

"Is there any more you can tell me?" said Reed.

"Not much," said Curly Joe. "Slim rode up to the shack early this morning. He was in pretty bad shape. We took him in and cleaned up his wound. He said that

Slocum had joined up with the army that Red was raising for Gould. His plan was to spy on them and get word to us whenever anything was about to happen. He told the boys what he had done, and he said for them to get back here and tell you. He went back into Wagon Gap and the boys headed back here. Along the way, someone shot Billy in the back and nicked Slim's arm. Slim rode hard all the way to the shack. Hell, I'd say he's lucky to have made it.''

"We're all lucky he made it," said Reed.

"Boss?" said Curly Joe.

"What is it?"

"What about Billy? I mean, he's just laying out there somewhere."

"There's nothing we can do about that just now," said Reed, a hard set to his jaw.

"It don't seem right," said Curly Joe.

"It's not right," said Reed. "It's wrong. It's wrong as all hell, and I hate it. But if this is going to be a war, we'll have plenty more to hate about it before we're done. Plenty more."

19

Gould, sided by Brady, Orren, and Smitty, went into the White Horse. The crowd was not large, for it was still early in the day, but it seemed to Gould like a proper-sized crowd for his purposes. He whispered to Marshal Brady, then went to his favorite table, Smitty right by his side. Brady moved to the center of the bar and asked the bartender for the use of his big wooden mallet. He pounded the bar several times to get the attention of all the customers.

"Gents," he said in his best booming voice, "I guess you all know that election day's coming on us right soon. Now I ain't going to spoil your time here with no campaign speeches, but I do hope you're all planning to vote for our fine mayor, Mr. Gould. Anyhow, he's just told me to get up here and announce that the next round is on him. That's right, friends. Drinks for everyone on Mayor Gould."

The cheer that went up from the crowd was much bigger than the size of the crowd seemed to justify, and everyone headed for the bar at once. Brady had to fight his way through in order to make his way, with bottle and glasses, back to the table where Gould and the two gunnies waited.

"A very good move, Mr. Mayor," he said as he sat down and offered the bottle to Gould. "And very well received, I'd say."

"Free booze always makes them cheer," said Gould. "It don't always mean they'll vote the right way."

"I've been making discreet inquiries of folks," Brady said, "and if they don't want to talk about it or indicate that they might be leaning in the wrong direction, I remind them in a gentle way that things can happen in the night. I think that most of them will come around to your side."

"They'd better," said Gould, "or we'll all be out of work around here."

"Hell," said Smitty, "what're you two worrying about anyhow? I remember last election the way you had them votes counted. You're going to win no matter how people votes."

"Shut up, you fool," snapped Gould.

"Well, no one can hear me."

"Just shut up and don't ever talk about that again," Gould said. He calmed then and lowered his voice. "That's a nasty business and best utilized only as a last resort. One always wants to win legitimately, if possible. But win nonetheless. Win at all costs."

He popped the cork and poured four glasses of whiskey. Lifting his glass, he said, "To the election. May the best man win."

Tobias Reed stood on his porch with a hard, stern expression on his weathered old face. His right hand held a Winchester, and his left arm was around the shoulders of his wife.

"He's got me playing his game, Myrtle," he said. "I ought to be out there talking to the voters, and he's got me making my home into an armed camp."

"What else can you do, dear?" Mrs. Reed said. "If he's importing an army of gunfighters, you have to be ready for them. They might try anything."

"I know that, but I'll be damned if I'll let him make me a prisoner on my own ranch."

He walked away from his wife to the edge of the porch and called out for Curly Joe. The cowboy came running to him.

"Yes, sir, Boss," said Curly Joe.

"Get me six good men," said Reed. "We're going out to campaign, and while we're out, you're in charge here."

Curly Joe turned to run, calling over his shoulder, "Yes, sir."

"Hold on there," Reed snapped. "I'm not through."

Curly Joe stopped and turned back around to face his boss.

"I said you'll be in charge, and you know what I meant by that."

"Yes, sir."

"I want you out here at all times keeping your eye on things," said Reed. "If I find out that you went into the house to see those two—women—even one time, even for one minute while I was away, I'll skin you alive. You understand me?"

"Yes, sir," said Curly Joe. "I surely do, and you can count on me, Boss."

"I'd better be able to," said Reed.

•   •   •

Slocum called a halt on the road when he spotted Billy's horse grazing contentedly off to the side, and then he knew that Billy was the one who had been shot. He caught up its trailing reins, then looked around.

"This is his horse," he said. "The body ought to be somewhere close by."

Merv rode a little farther down the road, and then he stopped.

"Hey," he called. "It's down here."

Leading the riderless horse, Slocum moved ahead toward Merv. Red followed. As he came up beside Merv, Slocum saw the body in the middle of the road. Until just this moment he had held out some small hope that Jasper Cummings might have lied to him about the killing, to goad him maybe. Or that maybe, even if Jasper had been telling the truth, the cowboy had not been killed. But there was the body up ahead in the road. Slocum urged his big stallion forward.

Near the body, he dismounted. He knelt and rolled it over gently. It was Billy. He couldn't allow himself to show too much concern. The two outlaws behind him wouldn't understand it. He straightened the body, then went back to Billy's horse and untied the blanket roll. He laid out the blanket there beside the body, and then he said quietly, "Give me a hand here."

Merv dismounted and came to Slocum's side. Together they laid the body on the blanket and folded the blanket over it. Then they lifted the bundle up onto the saddle of the dead man's horse and tied it down.

"Let's go," said Slocum.

Smitty was standing at the front window of the White Horse just a few feet from Gould's favorite table looking out onto the street. Gould, Orren, and Brady sat at the table. They hadn't been talking much and Smitty was bored. Besides, the other men had complained about Smitty's body odor, so he had decided to move away from them a short distance.

"Hey, Boss," he said.

"What?" Gould answered gruffly.

"Look at this."

"What is it?"

Brady got up and moved to the window.

"It's Tobias Reed," said Brady. "He's got six cow-hands with him. All heavily armed."

Gould got up so fast that he knocked his chair over. He rushed to the window to take a look. "What the hell's he up to?" he asked.

"Looks like he's looking for a fight," said Smitty.

"Where the hell's that goddamned Red?" Gould asked.

"What do you want us to do?" Brady asked.

"There's four of us and seven of them," said Gould. "What the hell can we do? Just keep your eye on them for now. That's all."

He went back to the table, righted his chair, and sat down again to pour himself a fresh whiskey. He sure didn't like the looks of that Running R gang in town. Reed himself and six armed cowboys. It had to mean trouble.

"What's going on out there?" he demanded.

"They tied up in front of Hogan's," said Smitty. "Dismounted."

"Looks like a crowd's gathering around them," said Brady.

"A crowd?" said Gould, jumping up again to move back to the window. "Hell," he said, "the son of a bitch is stumping. He's making a goddamned campaign speech.''

Gould headed for the front door of the White Horse with Brady, Orren, and Smitty right behind him. For all of his bulk, he almost ran across the street to where Reed was addressing a small crowd. As he drew closer, he could hear Reed's words.

"You all know me," Reed was saying. "I'm not a politician. I'm a rancher. But I've lived and worked in this county for most of my life, and I don't like what's been happening here in Joshville lately. I don't believe that you all like it either, and that's why I'm asking for your votes. If I'm elected your mayor, I promise you, we'll get to the bottom of the mess that things're in here, and we'll clean it up once and for all.''

"You talking about cleaning up the town," shouted Gould, "and you come in here with a whole gang of armed men behind you? What are you going to do? Run the mayor's office with gunfighters?''

"These are some of my cowhands," said Reed, "and yes, they're armed. The way things have been happening around here lately, I insisted that they be armed. There's a rumor going around, Gould, that you sent your man Red out to recruit more gunfighters for your own private army.''

"What? You must have made that rumor up your own self," said Gould. "You see any army around me? Where's my army? Marshal Brady here? Little old Orren? Smitty standing here stinking with cotton in his ears? That's one hell of an army, ain't it, folks? Why, if we was gathered here to fight instead of to debate political issues, your army would wipe us out in a minute.''

"We're not here for a fight, Gould," said Reed.

"It sure looks like it to me," Gould said. "What's it look like to you folks?"

No one in the crowd chose to respond to Gould's question, and the situation grew quiet and somewhat tense for a moment. Then someone in the crowd facing the road leading off toward Wagon Gap called out, "Look what's coming."

People scampered up onto Hogan's porch for a better look. Three riders were coming. One was leading a horse with what appeared to be a body slung across it. Gould moved out into the middle of the street away from the crowd. Brady, Orren, and Smitty followed. Gould squinted at the figures as they moved closer.

"Who is it?" he said.

"It's Red," said Smitty.

"Red?" Gould said. "With only two men? What the hell's wrong with him."

"One of them's Merv," said Smitty.

"Merv? Goddamn. Wait till I get my hands on that stupid Red."

"Other one looks like Slocum to me," said Brady. "Yeah. It's Slocum all right."

Gould didn't know what to think. He had sent Red out to raise an army, and here he was returning with only two men, and they were Merv and Slocum. Slocum was the very man who had destroyed Gould's gang of road agents, and Merv was the lone surviving member of that gang, the one he had ordered Red to kill to keep him quiet.

Red had to have turned on him. That was the only thing that made any sense. Otherwise he would not be bringing those two into town. Gould saw no help coming, only potential new problems. He had with him only Orren, Smitty, and Brady, none of them worth much in a pinch. And there was Reed with six armed cowboys. It looked bad.

"Brady," he said. "When they get on in here, bring Red over to my office. Alone."

He hurried on ahead. There was no time to waste. The thing that he dreaded most in life had happened. Everything he had worked so hard to build up in Joshville was collapsing around him, and if he didn't get out in a hurry, he would wind up in prison or at the end of a rope. But he did have cash. He had a lot of cash, and he could start over again someplace else, if he could just get out of town with the cash.

Slocum saw Reed there at Hogan's, so he steered his Palouse in that direction. When he reached the small crowd, he stopped and dismounted. He shot a glance at Red and Merv. "Stay here, boys," he said, and he walked over to Reed. "Mr. Reed."

"Slocum," said Reed.

"Mr. Reed, I've got some bad news for you. Billy was killed over by Wagon Gap."

"We heard," said Reed.

"Slim got away safe?"

"He was wounded," said Reed, "but he made it back. He'll be all right." He nodded toward the horse which was carrying the body. "Is that Billy?" he asked.

"Yes, sir," said Slocum. "It is."

"We'll take him home for burial," said Reed. "Slim told us you were coming back here with an army."

Slocum smiled slyly. He nodded over his shoulder toward Red and Merv. "That's it right there," he said. "That's my good news."

About then Brady walked up beside Red. "Gould wants to see you," he said. "In his office. Right now."

Red glanced at Merv, then over to Slocum, who was still in quiet conversation with Reed. "We'll be right along," he said.

"He don't want them," said Brady. "Just you."

Red knew that Gould would be furious. He had been looking for an army, and he wouldn't wait for a calm explanation. In fact, Red couldn't remember the reasons Slocum had used when he had talked him out of hiring more guns. He didn't want to face Gould alone, though. He knew that much.

And Gould had only Brady, Orren, and Smitty behind him. Red had Merv and Slocum. That gave him courage. Then there was this Running R gang and the crowd gathered around them. Red had no idea what that was all about, but it didn't look good. Of course, Slocum was talking to Reed, and he seemed to be getting along all right. It didn't appear as if the Running R was getting ready to fight anyone.

"Well," he said, "he don't get just me. Me and Merv and Slocum, we go together. Like I said, you can tell him we'll be along directly."

Brady looked like he wanted to say more, but instead he turned away in a huff and headed for Gould's office. As he passed by Smitty and Orren, he said, "Come on." Smitty started to follow, but Orren didn't move. Smitty hesitated.

"You coming?" he asked.

"Things looks pretty bad here to me," Orren said. "I reckon I'm pulling out." Orren turned without another word and headed for his horse. Smitty watched him for a moment, then raced after Brady.

About the same time, two of Reed's cowboys mounted up and started back toward the ranch, leading the horse that carried the remains of Billy. Slocum saw

Orren leaving, and pulled Reed a little further away out of the earshot of the crowd.

"Mr. Reed," he said, "the whole situation has changed here. Gould's down to just the four men you seen right here today, and they're a whole lot less than a first-rate outfit."

"Brady, Smitty, Red, and Merv," said Reed.

"That's it," said Slocum. "We could take them all right now. Real easy."

"It wouldn't be legal, Slocum," said Reed. "We need proof of wrong doing."

Slocum blew out a heavy sigh. "Red hired a man named Cummings over in Wagon Gap," he said. "It was Cummings that shot Billy and Slim. I killed Cummings."

"Proof, Slocum," said Reed. "Proof against Gould."

"Red admitted to me that they were behind the gang that was robbing the freight wagons."

"He could deny that he said that in court," said Reed. "It would be your word against his."

"Hey, Slocum," Red called out. "Gould wants to see us over in his office."

"All right, Mr. Reed," said Slocum. "I'll try to get your proof."

20

Gould was on his knees in front of the open safe when Brady and Smitty came into the office. He turned quickly with a six-gun in his hand.

"Don't shoot, Boss," said Smitty. "It's just me and the marshal. That's all."

"You assholes ever knock?" said Gould. "Where's that goddamn Red?"

"He said that the three of them would be along directly," said Brady.

"I said just Red," Gould snapped.

"That's what I told him," said Brady, "and he said if you get him, you get Merv and Slocum."

"It's that damned Slocum has got him acting that way," said Gould. "Red's got no guts on his own. Where the hell's Orren?"

"He lit out," said Smitty.

"Shit," said Gould. "You two stand outside the door. Don't let Slocum in here. Merv neither."

Smitty gave a nervous laugh.

"I ain't sure we can stop them," said Brady.

"There's a shotgun over there in the corner," said Gould. "Take that. It'll stop anything. Well, go on, damn you."

"Just one question, Mr. Mayor," said Brady.

"What, damn it?"

"It looks to me like you're fixing to clear out of here with all the money."

"Looks like that," said Smitty.

"*We're* fixing to clear out," said Gould. "So just keep Slocum out of here. And Merv. Slocum especially. Now go on. Hurry."

Brady got the shotgun, and he and Smitty went out of the office, closed the door, and took up positions on either side of it. They waited a couple of tense moments before Red showed up, flanked by Merv and Slocum. Brady leveled the shotgun and cocked it.

"What the hell's that for?" asked Red.

"I told you before," said Brady, "the boss wants to see you alone."

"Hell," said Slocum, "that's no problem. We'll wait for you over in the White Horse. Come on, Merv."

Red looked as if he wanted to go with Slocum and Merv, but he stood his ground. Soon he found himself alone, facing Brady's shotgun.

Brady grinned. "Go on in," he said. "Mr. Gould's waiting."

Smitty rapped on the door.

"What?" shouted Gould.

"Red's here."

"Send him in," said Gould. "Alone."

Smitty opened the door, and Red walked in. Gould was now sitting behind his desk. The revolver was on the desk in front of him beside a pair of stuffed saddle-bags.

"Shut the door behind you," Gould said, and Red shut the door. "I sent you to hire some men," Gould said. "Where are they?"

"I got Slocum and Merv," said Red.

"Slocum and Merv," Gould roared. "Slocum and Merv. I send you out for an army, and you come back with only two men, and of all men you could bring back here, you bring Slocum and Merv. You goddamn ignorant son of a bitch."

"Now, wait a minute, Boss," said Red. "Slocum, he's as good as five men at least. He took out that whole gang up at Bald Knob. Remember?"

"Oh, yes," said Gould. "Hell, yes, I remember. And it was *my* gang. Do you remember that?"

"He's a gunfighter," said Red. "He goes where the highest wages are. Whenever he took out that gang, we hadn't made him no offer. That's all. Over at Wagon Gap, I found this guy named Cummings."

"Not Jasper Cummings?"

"Yeah. It was Jasper."

"I've heard of him," said Gould. "He's good."

"Yeah," said Red. "I reckon he was, and it was him talked me into taking Slocum on. I didn't want to."

"Well, where's Cummings?" Gould asked.

"He killed one of Reed's cowboys, and Slocum killed Cummings."

"And that don't tell you what side Slocum's on? You ninny."

"No, Boss. Slocum said that Cummings was going to get us into a war with the Running R premature-like," said Red. "And besides that, Cummings was plotting to take over from you after we got here."

Gould held his head in his hands. "All right," he said. "All right. Shut up and let me think. I only know one thing. Slocum ain't with us. He suckered you. That's for sure. I ain't sure what he's up to, but he ain't with us. Now listen to me careful. We got to get out of town. I've got all the cash right here." He slapped the saddlebags on top of his desk, and Red's eyes opened wide. "Just you and me, Red," Gould continued. "I want you to get two good fast horses saddled up. Bring them around back just before dark. Wait for me there."

"What about Brady and Smitty and Merv?" said Red.

"Let me worry about them. Just do what I told you to do."

"Well, Merv and Slocum are waiting for me over at the White Horse," Red said.

"Go see them," said Gould. "Tell them I've calmed down, and I want to see each one of you one at a time. Tell Merv to come over next. Then go get the horses ready, but be careful and don't let no one see you."

"Right, Boss," Red said, and he hustled out the door.

"How'd it go?" Slocum asked as Red walked over to the table where Slocum and Merv waited in the White Horse.

"No problem," said Red. "He was hot at first, 'cause he was looking for a bunch of men, but I explained it to him the way you said it to me, and he calmed down. Right now I got to take Merv over there. After that he'll be wanting to talk to you, Slocum."

Slocum raised his eyebrows and looked from Red to Merv. "Sure," he said. "I'll be right here when you want me."

"Come on, Merv," said Red.

Merv got up and followed Red out of the White

Horse. Slocum watched them through the window until they reached Gould's office and went inside. He noticed Brady with the shotgun and Smitty still standing guard outside the door. Something was up, he decided, something that he was not being let in on. Red had never said so many words at a time before, and he had been stiff and a bit nervous saying them.

It seemed apparent to Slocum that Gould had not bought the story about Slocum switching sides, and he had drawn Red and Merv back into the fold. That wouldn't be difficult for anyone with a forceful personality to do, Slocum thought. He himself had persuaded Red not only to take him into his confidence but also to abandon the plan of raising an army. Red was easily swayed, and Merv would go along with whatever Red said.

But what was Gould up to now? So he didn't fall for Slocum's ruse. What was he planning to do about it? He couldn't possibly believe that he could put any of his four henchmen up against Slocum. Hell, Slocum thought, I could take all of them at the same time. He might try to plan some kind of ambush. Slocum would just have to watch his back. That's all.

Gould had seen himself outnumbered by less than half of Reed's crew, so he had to be feeling vulnerable. His plan had been to raise his strength, but with a little help from Slocum, Red had botched that one. Gould might try again, though. With Reed so damn set on doing everything according to the law, Gould might feel relatively safe. He might hole up in his office with three of those gunnies huddled around him, while the fourth one, probably Brady this time, made yet another run to Wagon Gap. Slocum decided that he would have to watch for that and stop any of the four who headed out of town.

What were the other possibilities? He could think of no other than the possibility that Gould, knowing that the game was up, might flee with whatever cash he had on hand. If he were to choose that option, the question would be whether he would try to slip away alone, abandoning his men, or whether he would take them along with him. Slocum suddenly wished that he had kept a few of Reed's cowboys in town with him. He couldn't afford to ride out to the ranch for them. Gould might pull something while he was gone. And there were just too many things to watch for for a man alone.

Slocum wished that he did not feel obligated to play by Reed's rules. It would be a fairly simple job to just take the five crooks, one or two at a time, until he had them all—dead or alive. That was the way that made sense to Slocum.

21

Slocum had been alone in the saloon for several hours, more than long enough to confirm his theory. Red would not be coming back to take him over for a talk with Gould. That had been nothing but a trick to get Merv away from Slocum, a ploy to leave Slocum alone. He had figured that at the time, but he had decided to just let it happen.

He was trying to decide what to do. He could sit by the window of the White Horse all night if necessary, he guessed. At least that way he could keep his eye on the front of Gould's office and keep track of the comings and goings of the gang. So far no one had gone anywhere. Brady and Smitty were still outside the door. The others, none of them, had come out of the office.

The front door of the White Horse swung open, and Slocum shot a glance in that direction to see who was coming in. He was surprised to see Curly Joe and three other cowboys. He noticed that Curly Joe looked around carefully, as if he wanted to be careful of who might see him talking to Slocum. Slocum waved a hand.

"Come on over, boys," he said.

Curly Joe jerked his head, and the other cowboys followed him over to where Slocum sat. "Is it safe?" Curly Joe asked.

"Sit down," said Slocum. He shoved a bottle toward Curly Joe. "Have a drink. And don't worry. They're on to me anyhow. I'm just sitting here watching Gould's office over there."

One of the cowboys went to the bar for some extra glasses.

"Why?" said Curly Joe. "What's up?"

"I don't know," said Slocum. "Gould's got four men left, and they ain't any of them anything to worry about much. Not unless they slip up behind you. Two of them's over there guarding the door."

"Brady and Smitty," said Curly Joe. The cowboy returned from the bar and passed the glasses around. Curly Joe poured.

"Gould and the others are inside," said Slocum. "They been in there all afternoon."

"What do you reckon they're up to?" Curly Joe asked.

"All I can do is guess," said Slocum, "but I think they know they're whipped. They can either send another man out to try to hire more gunhands, or they can just light out while the getting's good."

"While they think it's good," said Curly Joe. "I bet they're fixing to light out. I bet that's what them two horses is doing out back of Gould's office."

"Out back?" said Slocum. "Is there a back door to that place?"

"Sure is," said Curly Joe.

"We seen two horses out there when we was riding in," said a cowboy.

"Oh," said Curly Joe, "this here is Chad. These boys is Mike and Elmo."

"Howdy, boys," said Slocum.

"Listen, Slocum," said Curly Joe. "There's five of them and five of us. Hell, we can take them easy."

"Your boss don't want us gunning them without some proof of what they done," said Slocum. "What I think we need to do, now that I've got some help here, is we need to send someone around to watch the back-side of that office."

"I'll go," said Chad, and he tossed down the remainder of his drink and headed for the door.

"If anyone tries to leave," said Slocum, "don't do anything but come and tell us."

"Right," said Chad, and he hurried on out.

"Two horses, you say?" said Slocum.

"That's right," said Curly Joe.

"That sounds to me like three men're about to get run out on," said Slocum. "Wonder who's getting left behind."

They ordered beefsteak dinners and ate, and then Mike went to relieve Chad so that he could come back over to the White Horse for a meal. It was early evening.

"Well, look at that," said Slocum.

Merv had stepped out of the office and taken up a belligerent stance just in front of the door, between the other two men.

"Three of them's outside," said Curly Joe.

"Two men inside," said Slocum. "Two horses out back. Something's about to happen over there. Come on."

"Where we going?" Curly Joe asked.

They were all up and on the way to the door as Slocum answered, "You're going around back with Mike. I'm going to stir something up, with these boys backing me."

They went outside, and Curly Joe headed for the far end of the street to move around behind the buildings there. Slocum walked casually to a place directly across the street from the front door of Gould's office. He saw the three guards stiffen, ready for a fight.

"You two just stand here," he said to the cowboys. "Don't do anything unless those three over there start shooting at me."

He stepped down off the board sidewalk and moved slowly to the center of the street. Brady raised his shotgun.

"Hold it right there, Slocum," he said.

"I been waiting over here all day for Gould to send for me," said Slocum.

"Yeah?" said Brady. "Well, he ain't going to. Why don't you just get the hell out of town? Ain't nothing left for you here."

"Funny you should say that," said Slocum. "It seems to me like someone else is thinking about getting out of town."

"What the hell're you talking about?" Smitty asked.

"You all don't know about the two horses tied up out back?" Slocum asked.

"What two horses?" said Merv, looking at Brady.

"Ain't no horses out there," said Brady. "What're you trying to pull?"

"I ain't trying to pull nothing," said Slocum, "but someone is. There's two saddled horses out behind Gould's office, just waiting there. There's two men inside, ain't there? Gould and Red. And I'll bet that

Gould's got all his cash inside the office there, ain't he? It sure as hell looks to me like them two are going to be riding out of town with all that money while you three are left here like fools guarding an empty office."

"Merv," said Brady, "run around and take a look."

"Me?"

"Go on," said Brady. "Just take a look and get right back here."

"All right," said Merv, and he headed for the far end of the street.

"Well," said Slocum, "I'll leave you boys to work out your problems." He moved back to the walkway to join the two cowboys there. Some chairs were lined up against a storefront, and Slocum pulled one out and sat in it, leaning back against the wall. "Join me, fellows?" he said. The cowboys sat down, one on either side of Slocum. They stared together at Brady and Smitty across the way.

In another moment, Merv came running back to the front of the office. He hurried back to the side of Brady.

"There's two horses waiting out back, all right," he said. "What're we going to do?"

Brady hesitated only an instant, then made a quick decision.

"Come on," he said, and he jerked open the front door of the office and stepped boldly inside with the shotgun leveled. "Gould, you double-crossing son of a bitch," he snarled.

Gould reached for the six-gun on his desk top, and Brady pulled the trigger. The roar inside the small office was deafening. Smitty, who had come inside just behind Brady, screamed, grabbed his ears, and turned to run back outside. He ran into Merv. Gould, a bloody mess from the blast, flung up his arms wildly and fell back against the far wall. Red grabbed for the revolver at his side, but Brady swung the shotgun toward him, and Red turned and ran out the back door instead. Merv disentangled himself from Smitty to move up beside Brady as Smitty ran out the front door into the street.

"Where's the money?" said Merv.

Brady poked the barrel of his shotgun toward the saddlebags on the desk. "Check that," he said. Merv ran over to the desk and jerked open one side of the bags. He turned back toward Brady with a wide grin on his face. "Son of a bitch is full of money," he said. "Full."

Out back Red clambered aboard the nearest waiting horse, and was about to kick it into a run when Curly Joe stepped into his path with a cocked revolver in his hand.

"Going somewhere, Red?" he said.

Red jerked the horse around only to see Mike waiting for him there. He sat still and raised his arms high over his head.

As soon as he heard the shotgun blast, Slocum jumped up from his seat across the street from Gould's office and ran toward the fracas, pulling his Colt as he ran. The two cowboys followed him close behind. Just as they were about to reach the office door, Smitty came out holding his ears and whimpering.

Slocum grabbed Smitty's revolver, tossed it aside, and stepped quickly into the office. Brady whirled with the shotgun in hand, but he was too slow. Slocum fired, his bullet smashing into Brady's right shoulder. The crooked lawman cried out in pain, dropped the gun, and clutched at his bloody shoulder. Merv, his back to Slocum, still leaning over the desk, did not bother to turn, did not even straighten up. He only raised his hands.

"Don't shoot," he whined. "Don't shoot. I quit. Please don't shoot."

Slocum, accompanied by Curly Joe, Mike, Chad, and Elmo, rode up to Tobias Reed's big ranch house. Reed had heard their approach, and came out on the porch to meet them.

"It's all over, Mr. Mayor," said Slocum.

"What are you talking about?" said Reed.

"Gould's dead, and the folks in town got together and said they couldn't wait for election day," said Curly Joe. "They decided that you're the interim mayor, whatever that means. Come election day, they said, they'll make it even more official."

"That's what they said, Boss," said Chad.

"Damn it," snapped Reed. "I told you that we had to do everything according to the law. I told you not to go shooting the place up. Goddamn it to hell, I told you—"

"Just hold your horses, Reed," said Slocum. "We didn't do a damn thing. That bunch got to feuding among themselves. Brady killed Gould. All we did was just move in and put a stop to it."

"We locked them all up in the jailhouse," said Curly Joe, "all except of course for old Gould."

"Well, I'll be damned," said Reed. Mrs. Reed, Francine, and Jessie had come out onto the porch by this time, and Reed put an arm around his wife's shoulder. "It's over, Myrtle," he said. "Did you hear?"

"And the boss is the new mayor of Joshville," said Curly Joe.

"Slocum," said Reed, "there's a job here for you if you want it, either at the ranch or in town. Joshville's going to need a new marshal."

"Thanks, Mr. Reed," said Slocum, "but I think I'll be moving on. I would appreciate the loan of your line shack for another night."

"You've got it," said Reed, "for as long as you like."

"Thanks," said Slocum.

"Curly Joe," said Reed, "you and these other boys here take tomorrow off. You deserve it."

"Thanks, Boss," said Curly Joe.

"Yes, sir, Mr. Mayor," said Chad. "Thanks a heap."

"Well," said Jessie, "I guess it's safe enough for me and Francine to go back to town now. Mrs. Reed, we appreciate your hospitality."

"We were glad to have you here," Mrs. Reed said.

In a short time, the wagon was once again loaded with the belongings of Jessie and Francine, and Curly Joe was driving toward town. Chad, Mike, and Elmo rode ahead. Slocum turned off toward the line shack. Curly Joe looked at the two women.

"You in a big hurry to get back to Joshville?" he asked.

Jessie looked after Slocum, then looked at Francine. "I'm not in a hurry," she said. "How about you?"

"No hurry at all," said Francine.

Curly Joe turned the team to follow Slocum and whipped them up.

"Hey, Slocum," he shouted. "Wait for us. We're going to have us a celebration."

JAKE LOGAN

TODAY'S HOTTEST ACTION WESTERN!

__SLOCUM AND THE LADY 'NINERS #194	0-425-14684-7/$3.99
__SLOCUM AND THE PIRATES #196	0-515-11633-5/$3.99
__SLOCUM #197: THE SILVER STALLION	0-515-11654-8/$3.99
__SLOCUM AND THE SPOTTED HORSE #198	0-515-11679-3/$3.99
__SLOCUM AT DOG LEG CREEK #199	0-515-11701-3/$3.99
__SLOCUM'S SILVER #200	0-515-11729-3/$3.99
__SLOCUM #201: THE RENEGADE TRAIL	0-515-11739-0/$4.50
__SLOCUM AND THE DIRTY GAME #202	0-515-11764-1/$4.50
__SLOCUM AND THE BEAR LAKE MONSTER #204	0-515-11806-0/$4.50
__SLOCUM AND THE APACHE RANSOM #209	0-515-11894-X/$4.99
__SLOCUM'S GRUBSTAKE (GIANT)	0-515-11955-5/$5.50
__SLOCUM AND THE FRISCO KILLERS #212	0-515-11967-9/$4.99
__SLOCUM AND THE GREAT SOUTHERN HUNT #213	0-515-11983-0/$4.99
__SLOCUM #214: THE ARIZONA STRIP WAR	0-515-11997-0/$4.99
__SLOCUM AT DEAD DOG #215	0-515-12015-4/$4.99
__SLOCUM AND THE TOWN BOSS #216	0-515-12030-8/$4.99
__SLOCUM AND THE LADY IN BLUE #217 (4/97)	0-515-12049-9/$4.99

Payable in U.S. funds. No cash accepted. Postage & handling: $1.75 for one book, 75¢ for each additional. Maximum postage $5.50. Prices, postage and handling charges may change without notice. Visa, Amex, MasterCard call 1-800-788-6262, ext. 1, or fax 1-201-933-2316; refer to ad #202d

Or, check above books	Bill my: ☐ Visa ☐ MasterCard ☐ Amex _____ (expires)
and send this order form to:	
The Berkley Publishing Group	Card#_____
P.O. Box 12289, Dept. B	Daytime Phone #_____ ($10 minimum)
Newark, NJ 07101-5289	Signature_____
Please allow 4-6 weeks for delivery.	**Or enclosed is my:** ☐ check ☐ money order
Foreign and Canadian delivery 8-12 weeks.	

Ship to:

Name_____	Book Total	$_____
Address_____	Applicable Sales Tax (NY, NJ, PA, CA, GST Can.)	$_____
City_____	Postage & Handling	$_____
State/ZIP_____	Total Amount Due	$_____

Bill to: Name_____

Address_____ City_____

State/ZIP_____

If you enjoyed this book, subscribe now and get...

TWO FREE

A $7.00 VALUE—

If you would like to read more of the very best, most exciting, adventurous, action-packed Westerns being published today, you'll want to subscribe to True Value's Western Home Subscription Service.

Each month the editors of True Value will select the 6 very best Westerns from America's leading publishers for special readers like you. You'll be able to preview these new titles as soon as they are published, *FREE* for ten days with no obligation!

TWO FREE BOOKS

When you subscribe, we'll send you your first month's shipment of the newest and best 6 Westerns for you to preview. With your first shipment, two of these books will be yours as our introductory gift to you absolutely *FREE* (a $7.00 value), regardless of what you decide to do. If

you like them, as much as we think you will, keep all six books but pay for just 4 at the low subscriber rate of just $2.75 each. If you decide to return them, keep 2 of the titles as our gift. No obligation.

Special Subscriber Savings

When you become a True Value subscriber you'll save money several ways. First, all regular monthly selections will be billed at the low subscriber price of just $2.75 each. That's at least a savings of $4.50 each month below the publishers price. Second, there is never any shipping, handling or other hidden charges—*Free home delivery*. What's more there is no minimum number of books you must buy, you may return any selection for full credit and you can cancel your subscription at any time. A TRUE VALUE!

A special offer for people who enjoy reading the best Westerns published today.

WESTERNS!

NO OBLIGATION

Mail the coupon below

To start your subscription and receive 2 FREE WESTERNS, fill out the coupon below and mail it today. We'll send your first shipment which includes 2 FREE BOOKS as soon as we receive it.

Mail To: **True Value Home Subscription Services, Inc. P.O. Box 5235**
120 Brighton Road, Clifton, New Jersey 07015-5235

YES! I want to start reviewing the very best Westerns being published today. Send me my first shipment of 6 Westerns for me to preview FREE for 10 days. If I decide to keep them, I'll pay for just 4 of the books at the low subscriber price of $2.75 each; a total $11.00 (a $21.00 value). Then each month I'll receive the 6 newest and best Westerns to preview Free for 10 days. If I'm not satisfied I may return them within 10 days and owe nothing. Otherwise I'll be billed at the special low subscriber rate of $2.75 each; a total of $16.50 (at least a $21.00 value) and save $4.50 off the publishers price. There are never any shipping, handling or other hidden charges. I understand I am under no obligation to purchase any number of books and I can cancel my subscription at any time, no questions asked. In any case the 2 FREE books are mine to keep.

Name _____

Street Address _____ Apt. No. _____

City _____ State _____ Zip Code _____

Telephone _____

Signature _____
(if under 18 parent or guardian must sign)   **12030-8**

Terms and prices subject to change. Orders subject
to acceptance by True Value Home Subscription
Services, Inc.

First in an all-new series from the creators of Longarm!

BUSHWHACKERS

They were the most brutal gang of cutthroats ever
assembled. And during the Civil War, they sought justice
outside of the law—paying back every Yankee raid with one
of their own. They rode hard, shot straight, and had their
way with every willin' woman west of the Mississippi. No
man could stop them. No woman could resist them. And no
Yankee stood a chance of living when Quantrill's Raiders
rode into town...

Win and Joe Coulter become the two most wanted men in
the West. And they learn just how sweet—and deadly—
revenge could be...

Coming in July 1997
BUSHWHACKERS by B. J. Lanagan
0-515-12102-9/$5.99
Look for the second book in September 1997
BUSHWHACKERS #2: REBEL COUNTY
also by B. J. Lanagan 0-515-12142-8

VISIT THE PUTNAM BERKLEY BOOKSTORE CAFÉ ON THE INTERNET:
http://www.berkley.com/berkley

Payable in U.S. funds. No cash accepted. Postage & handling: $1.75 for one book, 75¢ for each
additional. Maximum postage $5.50. Prices, postage and handling charges may change without
notice. Visa, Amex, MasterCard call 1-800-788-6262, ext. 1, or fax 1-201-933-2316; refer to ad #705

Or, check above books	Bill my: ☐ Visa ☐ MasterCard ☐ Amex _____ (expires)
and send this order form to:	
The Berkley Publishing Group	Card#_____
P.O. Box 12289, Dept. B	Daytime Phone #_____ ($10 minimum)
Newark, NJ 07101-5289	Signature_____

Please allow 4-6 weeks for delivery.   **Or enclosed is my:** ☐ check ☐ money order
Foreign and Canadian delivery 8-12 weeks.

Ship to:

Name_____	Book Total	$_____
Address_____	Applicable Sales Tax	$_____
	(NY, NJ, PA, CA, GST Can.)	
City_____	Postage & Handling	$_____
State/ZIP_____	Total Amount Due	$_____

Bill to: Name_____

Address_____City_____

State/ZIP_____